Acknowledgement

I want to thank my wife Edith Ingenhaag for her artistic point of view.

Randy Cribbs for his hard work and skills that made this book a reality, and

My sister, Dr. Florence Wood for her encouragement, time and editing.

Dedication

To my children Colleen and Victor.

Their love and inspiration has kept me focused on the IS

Everything

Is

Victor Rugg

With Randy Cribbs

EVERYTHING IS

EVERYTHING IS connected. EVERYTHING IS forever. Mass and energy cannot be destroyed, only changed or rearranged. Mass and energy are either sentient or incognitive. All sentient beings align along a range from the negative to positive IS. Our DNA is found to some extent, everywhere in the universe. On some planets, it has become dangerously diluted, causing an ominous shift toward the negative IS.

It is time all sentient beings connect to positive IS.

Jebumo
The Planet Plytar

PROLOGUE

"The time has come to intervene."

The speaker, though he did not actually verbalize because of the telepathic capabilities of their species, glanced at the others suspended around him.

"Jebumo, do you not believe they will evolve to the better if left alone?"

"I do not. Their DNA is too corrupt and we risk it spreading to other planets if action is not taken."

"But their civilization has evolved so quickly, surely more time is needed. Intervention must be a final resort. It is our way," the challenger replied, unconvinced.

Jebumo glanced at the speaker. "This world, Earth, is stressed by war and 0economic hardship. New diseases plague the planet and their knowledge base is not keeping up. We have all watched the impact of global warming in the dramatic shifts that are causing horrific storms and temperature changes. The situation is caused in large part by the inhabitants, but they are unwilling to make the sacrifices required to reverse the damage. They are more interested in arguing over solutions than implementing them."

He gestured toward the spinning planet and continued. "Some leaders are struggling to come up with answers, but their efforts are countered by a handful of powerful humans who are driven by power, greed, and profit. That has caused many of the planet's ills. I must also note that while their space exploration programs are far behind other planets, many non-government enterprises are making significant progress. Their motivation is profit and they are unhampered by government obstacles. With their successes, we risk the possibility their bad DNA will spread. These private sector space programs are funded by the same humans responsible for pollution."

"You are convinced they will not right their course?" another in the group asked.

Jebumo replied, "I am. And because dozens of their countries have nuclear arsenals, the possibility of a nuclear strike, and retaliation is significant. There are countries at war constantly and others in a perpetual state of turmoil. Issues of the poor and middle classes are not addressed, which almost certainly will result in civil wars. This is in fact happening now in some places. This race has always been prone to violence, and the masses, who are arming themselves at an alarming rate, will not accept their deteriorating situation forever."

Jebumo looked around again. "We must change the situation before the planet implodes."

"Did we plant a seed?" one of the group asked.

"Yes, Sirta was sent, and the son of her offspring has evolved to the necessary condition."

2

"Sirta should speak," said Gonda, a senior advisor.

Even as Gonda had thoughts of Sirta, her form began to materialize among the suspended group.

"Sirta, as I recall, you spent more time than usual on earth planting your seed, and now Jebumo thinks we need an intervention. Do you agree?" Gonda asked.

Sirta addressed his comments in order. "I felt it necessary to stay on earth longer, so I could meld with the offspring of my offspring, John Klein. These humans have gone through generations of deviant and violent behavior. Their corrupt DNA is strong. To ensure our mission, I wanted to be personally involved with John Klein's early years to insure the dominance of our DNA. I feel confident this has happened."

"I agree with you. This is a greedy, violent lot. They worship the rich and powerful and seem to care little for others. Even in what seems to be for some their constant pursuit of happiness, most place themselves at the center of their efforts. They just don't seem to understand. Are they even worth this mission?" one of the other beings asked.

Sirta responded immediately. "Yes, they are. Many humans have a basic goodness about them. They want to do right, but there are so many others with corrupt DNA, it is very difficult for them. John Klein, and others like him, have come to understand that true happiness comes through helping others who for different reasons are not able to help themselves.There is enough good left for an intervention to succeed, but we must move quickly."

They all looked to the senior advisor, who had been listening to the exchanges.

"The earthlings seem to be difficult to define collectively. They are scattered around the planet, and though they have evolved technology that connects them, they are very different in many ways. What they do have in common is a warring nature. We have watched their evolution and that has become clear."

He glanced at Sirta and continued.

"I do agree with Sirta. There are still many who chose to put others before themselves. The earthling chose for Sirta's seeding was among those. Their numbers, however, are growing smaller. For those reasons, I agree with the intervention."

"And has contact been made?" One of the other figures asked.

"No, but the seed of Sirta is in John Klein. He has been willed to act, and has the resources to succeed."

As the images and voices projected from earth dissipated, the group simply vanished, signifying agreement.

CHAPTER ONE

CHANGE

On Tuesday evening, something happened that affected the entire solar system. A slight skip in the layer of a black hole caused a pause in the space time continuum. It became Tuesday morning again, and everything reverted to the way it had been. The day did not happen.

Consummated projects, months or years in the making were no longer finalized. Broken arms and legs were whole again, brides were virgins, and those who had died breathed again. No one knew beforehand what the day held, the day that had already passed, and that everything that had happened would happen again, with one exception.

That morning, billionaire John Klein suddenly announced his retirement and revealed plans to travel and relax. The solar system skip was purposefully created to reverse that decision when Sirta realized what he had done.

Klein was needed in his position of power and in his original frame of mind to execute their intervention plan.

Though a drastic move, it was decided after much debate, that this was the most reasonable recourse available; a do-over. Now, it only remained to be seen whether or not Sirta's entry into Klein's subconscious mind would get the plan back on track.

Klein sat hunched over on the side of his bed thinking about a weird dream. One of those dreams that seemed very real yet could not possibly be. He glanced at the clock: TUESDAY 7:00 A. M. It took a moment for his mind to register that information.

That's impossible, he thought, it should be Wednesday, not Tuesday.

He turned the television to his favorite morning news channel. The caption above the talking heads so-called news verbiage showed Tuesday, 7:02 A.M. Switching to another channel, he discovered the same thing.

He thought again about his strange dream and his sudden decision to retire. Had he made a mistake? Dropping out, abandoning a secret goal he harbored for many years. Somehow, he felt the answer was yes. This was not like him, second guessing, but somehow it just didn't feel right.

His thoughts were interrupted by the ringing phone.

"John Klein."

"John, just a reminder, we have the big board meeting this morning," his executive secretary said.

"Board meeting? We did that yesterday."

"No John, it's today."

He made no reply.

"John, are you all right?"she asked when he did not respond.

"Yes, yes, of course." He paused, then added, "Did I make any announcements yesterday?"

"Well, no. What kind of announcement?"

John thought about the dream again. He glanced at the TV, showing scenes of the civil war in Syria.

"John, are you there?"

He jerked back to the present. "Yes, I'm here. Cancel the board meeting. I have something important to do," he blurted.

"Okay. You're the boss."

As John hung up the phone, he suddenly felt that his life had clarity again. His thoughts turned to a meeting quite different from the canceled board meeting.

PART I

PRESENT DAY

CHAPTER TWO

A DAY IN THE LIFE

John Klein called New York his home, even though he had apartments in Paris, Rome, Berlin, London and a spread in St. Croix. He was born to a wealthy New York City family and as a small boy vacationed in the Hamptons.

Though he could live in any of the several buildings he owned in New York, he preferred an old prewar building between 56th and 57th Street on Park Avenue where he occupied the penthouse. In the summer he could be found at a summer cottage, a 12,500 square-foot affair designed by Francis Fleetwood, on Georgica Pond in East Hampton.

Klein was one of the wealthiest men in the world, if not the wealthiest, but he was able to keep his name off the Forbes list of wealthiest people by owning everything through multiple corporations that could not be traced to his name. He liked it this way, because at 70 years old, he was getting ready to embark on the most important investment of his life.

He was married and had two children. His wife rarely spent any time with him because of the demands of her wellness center in Lake Mary, Florida, and its satellite in Costa Rica. His wife studied yoga many years ago at the Omega Institute in Rhinebeck, New York, and became engrossed with organic foods and homeopathic medicine.

When she told John she wanted to open up the center, he wrote her a check. She tried for many years to create in John an understanding of the wisdom of being a vegetarian and eating organic foods. Finally, she realized it was hopeless and moved on. They still loved each other very much and he would visit her from time to time, but when his taste for meat became too strong, he left.

His son never showed much interest in business and was satisfied living in Aspen where he ran the family charitable trust. He was content giving away money rather than making it. He loved Colorado because it offered him the outdoor life he craved. His mountain bike and snowboard were always at the ready. He was married and had a beautiful daughter who by age five was already skiing. His wife worked with him in the arduous task of giving away millions of dollars of John's money each year.

They initially thought that this would be easy, but later found the business of philanthropy to be complicated, requiring a staff of 25 people to pour over applications and make recommendations.

In some ways, John envied his son who, though always a good student and hard worker, had from a very young age insisted on 'doing his own thing'. Simply enjoying life was far more important to him than becoming famous or rich. His job running John's charities was difficult, but it afforded him the opportunity to play and enjoy his family. John was delighted the situation worked out the way it did. His son, whom he trusted implicitly, managed the funds while enjoying his life.

His daughter lived in California where she ran her own public relations company focusing on social marketing. John had wanted her to work for him but, like him, she was very independent and decided to go it alone, becoming very successful. His relationship with his children was close and he saw them whenever he could.

John was the third in a succession of savvy businessmen, starting with his grandfather, John Klein. He had made most of his fortune backing new inventions and subsequently managing the production and marketing of many. Both John's grandfather and father, the second and third John's, continued expanding the Klein business empire until today, under John IV, it was global.

Though the Klein ancestry was impressive, John Klein I was in fact not his biological grandfather.

John's true grandfather, though unknown to him for many years, was the famous inventor Nikola Tesla, who came to America in 1884. He was never married, preferring to avoid emotional entanglements, and lived alone most of his life. How he came to father a child was preordained.

One of Tesla's female assistants, Sirta, was sent to Earth from another planet, a fact unknown to Tesla. This is where a process that would change the world began.

Sirta was very beautiful. Perfect body contours, with long red hair and green eyes. Tesla was amazed at her intellect and ability to understand the work they were doing. In fact, she was always guiding and expanding their research. What Tesla did not know was that Sirta was part of a grand plan to lay the groundwork to one day save our planet should that become necessary. This plan had been set into motion many years ago when beings on the planet Plytar recognized we were evolving to disaster.

Sirta was sent to Earth to mate with Tesla, but this proved to be more difficult than anticipated.

Even though Sirta was a beautiful and desirable woman in human form, Tesla was interested in one thing only—his work. After employing every lady-like charm in her power, all to no avail, it became obvious that this kind, brilliant man simply could not, or would not comprehend her sexual interest in him. She finally decided that she had to employ the sexual methodology of Plytar if a mating was ever to occur.

Tesla arrived at his lab early one morning, surprised that Sirta was already at work. She was adjusting a new high voltage generator they were designing. Tesla was not aware that she had significantly amped up the machine to an incredible amount of voltage.

As Tesla entered, Sirta grabbed the terminals and an extreme amount of electricity began passing through her body. Alarmed, Tesla grabbed her in an attempt to break her body free of the charge. Instead, the voltage increased and they both began glowing as their bodies became one. Sirta took charge as the form of cosmic foreplay caused Tesla, possibly for the first time in his life, to become overwhelmed with sensuality. They made passionate love and lay exhausted as Sirta slowly caused the voltage to lower so Tesla's body would not be harmed.

When he regained his senses, Tesla inquired about Sirta's health and discovering she was fine, gave her a stern lecture about being more careful.

He had no recollection of what had transpired.

From this union would come a child named John. Knowing Tesla's lifestyle and that he would never marry, Sirta married John Klein Senior within days of her conception. She never told her husband he wasn't the father of John Junior. The deceptive nature of this entire ruse was a necessary evil because Tesla was a brilliant man who possessed the DNA that would subsequently allow his offspring the ability to save the world.

Not until January 8, 1943, the day after Tesla died, did Sirta come forward with the truth.

In his lifetime, Tesla had received over 700 patents worldwide for his inventions, which included the air conditioner. In 1886, he invented the very first transmitter and was credited for inventing the radio. In 1888, he invented the first remote-controlled boat.

He was quite revered in his day and was friends with such notables as J.P. Morgan, Astor, and Westinghouse to name a few. In fact, Westinghouse bought many of Tesla's inventions, including the motors and transformers that were used in the first hydroelectric plant that Tesla invented and installed at Niagara Falls in 1895.

He built his largest laboratory in Colorado Springs and through experiments conducted there, realized that electric current could be sent through the airways.

Interested, Westinghouse also supplied the capital for Wharton Cliff, a project in Shoram, Long Island. It was a tower, 187 feet high, built between 1901 and 1905. The idea was that unlimited amounts of energy could be produced and sent through the airwaves to power ships, buildings, etc. Tesla felt it could also potentially be used for interplanetary communications.

The tower was torn down when Westinghouse pulled his money because a usage meter could not be connected to the process for financial gain. Many experts felt if it had been finished and worked, the world would be a much cleaner and safer place to live.

This wasn't the only time Shoram found itself in controversy. Many years later, a nuclear plant was built there by the local power company, LILCO, for over a billion dollars, but was never opened because of safety concerns.

John Klein always wanted to continue his grandfather's work. He had many of his drawings and notes and studied them all of his life.

When time permitted, he would sit for hours leafing through page after page of ideas and theories written in Tesla's unique, hurried scrawl. The penmanship suggested a man whose mind was filled with ideas; so many that his hand could not convert his thinking to written words fast enough. The end result on many pages was cryptic marks that only resembled words. With time, John had become adept at deciphering Tesla's unique code for words and phrases, developed no doubt as a time saving measure to capture the barrage of ideas spilling from his mind.

Some of his ideas defied imagination, yet on close scrutiny could not be viewed as impossible. Others had evolved to fruition, most by Tesla's guiding hand, others by enterprising scientists after his time.

The idea of interplanetary communication interested John the most. He often thought that Wardenclyffe was an amazing idea, especially when it came to communicating with other planets. His secret goal was to build it someday. He could not explain his interest in this goal, but it was never out of his mind. It was as if a seed had been planted and continued to grow.

In the meantime, when John drove the Tesla car named after his grandfather each time he was in the Hamptons, and listened to the rock band that chose Tesla as its name, the seed grew larger.

* * *

Several weeks after his strange dream, on July 2, John got up at 6 AM as usual but the day would not be a workday. John was refocused on the dream that simply would not leave his mind. Today, the final step to attaining that goal, the last phase of his plan, started in earnest. He was going to *Bayberry*, his estate on Georgica Pond for the Fourth of July weekend.

He had a very special party planned for the Fourth and had enlisted several unwitting accomplices, including his neighbor and friend Ron Perlman, who was making his several guest cottages available.

Elton John would sing for a million dollars. His other neighbor, Steven Spielberg, promised to deliver some very special guests which usually turned out to be famous stars. Sort of tit-for-tat since John had bankrolled a number of blockbusters for Spielberg over the years.

It was imperative that certain people attend the party to accommodate John's plan. Their presence at a subsequent meeting was critical and the attendance of a who's who party list would assure that.

15

CHAPTER THREE
CONFIDANT

Jebumo, with Gonda, a Plytar senior advisor beside him, watched Sirta materialize.

"You mentioned an intervention in your communiqué, so I asked Gonda to join us," Jebumo said.

"Of course," Sirta replied. "I know we do not like to involve more than one being on a planet being transformed, but I believe we need to make an exception with the Earth mission."

"But you have a seed in place with this John Klein, and his plan is underway," Gonda said.

"Yes, I do. But the humans are different."

"How so?" Jebumo asked.

"They can be brutal and unforgiving in their dealings with each other, and their psyche does not thrive well in isolation. There are other humans who will try to stop John Klein."

"But he has our DNA," the adviser stated.

"That is true, but he is also part human, with their peculiar frailty and needs. Humans need confidants, particularly when under great pressure. I learned this during my time on earth."

"You are connected to his mind?" Gonda asked.

"Yes, but this is different," she replied.

Gonda was silent for a moment. "Did we not do a timeshift for this earth because Klein strayed from the mission?"

"Yes, we did, and he is now focused, but some of these humans are very corrupted and powerful. They will go to extremes to achieve what they want— we know this. We need a preventive measure in place to accommodate Klein's human need to share."

Jebumo waved his arm toward the screen and scenes from Earth appeared. He waved again and John Klein filled the screen, gazing out his office window as if in a daze. "What would you have us do?"

"I wish to cause him to bring another human into his confidence and share his plan. His friend and employee, Viktor."

"The more beings involved in a transformation plan, the more chance of failure. You know this," Gonda quickly said.

"I know, but with the humans...." She looked at the screen. "I believe he will need help; what they call moral support," she added.

"Moral support. Yes. These humans are so dependent on each other, yet they have evolved a culture of suspicion and distrust. It is very confusing." Gonda replied.

"I agree. There are close, caring families of earthlings who trust each other. There are others, within families and in their dealings with others professionally who do not operate on any level of trust. It was not always this way, but it is now the prevailing attitude." Sirta responded.

"You can influence Klein to trust this other human, but what if that trust is misplaced? It risks the mission." Gonda, unconvinced, retorted.

"Viktor is a good human. His actions suggest good DNA." She paused. "I'm certain he will prove his loyalty to Klein and benefit the mission.

Gonda looked at Jebumo and shrugged.

"Very well," he conceded.

The three figures faded away.

CHAPTER FOUR

GROUNDWORK

John dressed in a blue button-down shirt, tan slacks, and loafers without socks. He always dressed simply which made it easy for him to shop for himself. As the elevator opened on the ground floor, he was greeted by Max the doorman.

"Good morning, Mr. Klein— you look quite relaxed today."

"Thanks Max. I'm off to the Hamptons for a short break. What's new with you?" John said, giving Max his daily opportunity to fill him in on the news.

"You see that article about the woman who worked for McDonald's for ten years and still makes less than nine bucks an hour?" Not waiting for a response, Max continued, "She shows up at a big meeting the CEO had and asked him if he thought that was fair. The woman's raising two kids and working full-time for peanuts, and corporate America does not want to share. I don't know what's going on, Mr. Klein."

"The economy is definitely a little shaky right now, Max. That's for certain."

"Now, Mr. Klein, you're a rich guy. But I see in the news all the time where you give lots of dough to people and charity deals. Problem is that most of those big rich corporations don't do that. They pretend to, but they just keep getting bigger and bigger and schmucks like me in the middle class keep seeing our bucks do less."

"Well, the middle class is definitely the heartbeat of the country, Max."

"Yeah, I'm just not sure where the middle class is headed, Mr. Klein. Taxes have gotten ridiculous, and the government gives a check to everyone except us in the middle class. Big corporations, unions, and power groups own the government because they pay to get their boys elected and then get paid back. Hell, even if a guy is honest when he's elected to the hill, he either turns bad or he's out for not playing. I tell you, it's frustrating. I've got two kids in school, a mortgage and debts up to my eyeballs, and the government shuts down every few years, giving the bureaucrats a free vacation because they can't even talk to each other up there. And now we got the IRS going after people for what they believe and the Justice Department suing or charging people because of political views."

Max stopped his venting and took a deep breath. "Sorry, Mr. Klein, guess I'm just letting things get to me. The government just doesn't seem to have a handle on things. I read they've printed eighty-five billion bucks a month just to keep up, which they ain't doing. I worry about what my kids face down the road."

"You're right, Max. I agree with you." John paused. "Max, I'd be happy to loan you a few bucks."

"Mr. Klein, in all these years that I have known you, have I ever taken your money? I'm not about to start now. We'll figure this out. I know you're very powerful and influential so maybe you could get together with your friends and see what you can do about the middle class before it's too late. You know we're the engine that runs the economy and we're slowly running out of steam. If we go, it *all* goes."

"I know, and believe me when I tell you, I *am* working on it," John replied.

"Thanks Mr. Klein, and have a great weekend. Oh yeah—the Yanks won last night!"

"It's sure about time, right? Thanks, Max. You take care of yourself. I'll see you later."

John approached a Jaguar 120, one of his favorite cars.

"Hello John," the driver, Viktor, said as he moved toward John with the air of someone seeing an old friend.

"Are we ready, Viktor?".

"Of course we are. This will be the best party you ever had."

Viktor had become quite close to John over the years. Though John would never tell Viktor directly how to invest his money, and Viktor would never ask, John hoped that he'd been listening when he gave orders to buy and sell over the phone. In fact, Viktor listened well and was now worth about fifty million dollars, but would never stop driving for John.

Viktor was well-educated and had sold his business when he was fifty-one to set sail in the Caribbean. He sailed for thirteen months from Tortola to Venezuela and back to Palm Beach Gardens. When he returned, he sold his house in Sag Harbor, kept his house in East Hampton, and bought a house in Florida.

He now split his time between Florida and East Hampton, spending six months in both places. He had evolved into a professional photographer and when the East Hampton Star asked him to cover the annual garden tour several years ago, he agreed. That led to his first meeting with John.

As it turned out, Bayberry was on the tour because it had the most beautiful gardens in the Hamptons. Mr. Klein greeted the tour group and went on to describe the many different plantings. He noticed Viktor taking pictures and introduced himself. Viktor told him he was with the Star and all of his images would be of the plantings only and none of the house. Mr. Klein was impressed with Viktor's understanding of how important it was to keep his privacy for security reasons. Soon the conversation turned to security and John asked Viktor if he knew someone who would be interested in being his chauffeur and bodyguard.

"With all due respect, do you think I'm the one you should be asking? I mean, we just met. Don't you have an administrative assistant who could do some research and get recommendations?"

John laughed. "I have found in life that sometimes instinct and going by the seat of your pants works best. I need a local here in the Hamptons, one not tainted by the City. I would do the appropriate background check of course, but very often locals have given me great advice so that's why I'm talking to you. Also, I appreciate that you were sensitive to security on my property."

Viktor said, "Let me have your phone number and I'll get back to you tomorrow." The men parted with a hearty handshake and good eye contact.

The next day Viktor called as he had promised and they met at the Montauk Yacht Club for lunch. Viktor told him he would take the job and advised that he had a license for his Beretta, though he seldom carried it, and his driver's license was clean.

"Why do you have a gun license?" John asked.

"I sometimes carry large amounts of cash, and it's a good precaution to have extra protection. I was a marksman in the military during the Vietnam War and am not opposed to using it if I had to. It has never been fired except at the shooting range. My wife hates it."

"So, why do you want to be my driver? You're a photographer."

"Well, I have done many different things in my life and love new experiences and challenges. I'm only considering this because it is *you* I would be working for."

"You would be the most well educated and traveled driver I have ever had. Let's give it a try and see what happens."

That was fourteen years ago, and needless to say the two men had become great friends. Yet Viktor knew his place. Even though he was quite wealthy now, he was not a billionaire and never went to the big parties with Spielberg, Perlman, Askoff, Loren, Patricoff, etc. He didn't have any problem with that because he wouldn't like being with them very much anyway.

Over the years, the conversations in the car, when it was just the two of them, ran the full gamut from philosophy to economics. John discovered early on that Viktor was not the least bit interested in discussing politics. John followed politics out of necessity because few issues or events happened that didn't impact some part of his business empire.

On one of their excursions, John had asked Viktor his opinion on a bill being debated in the senate. Victor immediately became uncomfortable, evidenced by his reply.

"John, I have to show my ignorance by saying I don't know anything about it."

Because Viktor was knowledgeable in many areas, John was very surprised. "Well, guess you don't have an opinion then."

"I'll tell you John, there was a time I followed all the political going-on's. Watched the news and read newspapers routinely, but I just got tired of it. I never even watch the news anymore, except local morning shows so I can get the weather."

"So you don't tune in news channels every now and then just to see what's going on?"

"No, just the weather. I think the time when news was about just reporting the facts is over. To me, news, print and media, is biased and misleading. Every outfit in the game tries to jam their political leanings down our throat. If information doesn't support their political persuasion, they simply leave it out or slant it. They tailor their reporting to fit their biases. I decided I just didn't want to deal with it anymore."

"I guess I can't argue with you on that point. I actually pay a retired journalist friend of mine to prepare and send to me a daily report that 'fills in the gap' with the rest of the story." He chuckled. "It is astounding how all the facts change the reported story in a lot of cases. So, what do you watch on television?"

"Well, I did watch History Channel often, but even that depresses me these days, through no fault of their own."

"How so?"

"I love their programming, but when I watch shows I really enjoy, about the way things were, or the amazing accomplishments our ancestors had as they went about building this country, it saddens me that we seem to have let it all slip away."

He shot a glance at John through the rear view mirror. "Maybe I'm turning into a radical, John."

"No, not at all, Viktor. I understand your frustrations. Things definitely need fixing." He paused. "You remember my good friend Juliet Papa?"

"Definitely. One of the top reporters at 1010 WINS radio station. Great station, and I listen to Juliet all the time; me and millions of others."

"I had this idea for an all positive news station, and I wanted her to run it. She would be a fantastic fit."

John smiled as he thought of his friend Juliet. He always had a little crush on her. And why not. Extremely intelligent, beautiful thick hair, an amazing smile and vibrant personality.

"Anyway," John continued, "it would be simulcast all over the world, based right here in New York with antennas on top of the new World Trade Center. The charter would be to report only positive news stories. Could even expand to television. Just think of the people, like yourself, who have tuned out the media because of the slanted, negative coverage. If they had the option to tune in a station where they knew only positive stories were covered, I believe they would love it."

"I know I would." Viktor responded.

25

"Well, Juliet is thinking about it. At least she hasn't said no." He gave Viktor a glance. "So what do you watch?"

"Hardly any network T.V. because the commercials make me crazy. Many are simply a lie on their face, and others insult my intelligence. As a matter of fact, I think they are probably driving routine viewers insane, but they don't know it yet." He swerved the car skillfully to avoid an impatient driver. "Believe it or not, I watch a lot of sports. The thing with sports is that it's a game. Not serious. Nothing getting blown up, no talking heads telling us what they think we should hear. Any bias put forth before the game is put to rest when the contest unfolds before our eyes. Simple competition. May sound crazy since most people get excited watching a sporting event, but I actually relax. Weird, huh."

"No. Matter of fact, maybe I'll try it."

They both laughed, and since that time they avoided politics as much as possible and talked about art instead. John quickly realize that Viktor was very well read when it came to economics, and he listened carefully to whatever Viktor said after he predicted the tech and housing bubble. John had also seen this coming and positioned himself to make millions shorting the market.

For Viktor this was the best way to spend his time. His wife was a yoga instructor and into holistic medicine and developed a friendship with John's wife, who was now helping her manage the two centers. This worked perfectly for John because Viktor could be called up at a moment's notice. Viktor lived in a small cottage by the water on John's property and rented his house to a charming couple.

Today, as always, Viktor walked John to the car, looking right and left to make sure his flanks were covered. John was about 5 foot six and Viktor was 6 foot one with a big frame and broad shoulders. He was always an imposing figure wherever he went and John felt very safe with him.

He shut John's door, got behind the wheel and they were off down Park Avenue, right on 58th, and then another right on Second Avenue on their way to the Midtown Tunnel. John loved cars and preferred them to planes and helicopters, both of which he found too noisy. They knew if they left before twelve they could make it to East Hampton in a couple of hours. As they made their way through the tunnel and onto the Long Island Expressway, the traffic was light and Exit 70 seemed to come up faster than usual. Before long, they were on the Sunrise Highway with no traffic in sight.

Their light conversation was interrupted by John's ringing cell phone.

"John Klein."

John listened a moment, then said. "Who's handling it?"

He listened again.

"Who's he dealing with?" he asked.

Glancing at the rear view mirror, Viktor saw John roll his eyes and deducted what news he was receiving.

"Tell him to settle." He listened briefly, then spoke again. "I understand, Frank, and your concerns about setting a precedence is noted, but I have my reasons."

John heard out the appeal being made, then replied. "You're right, Frank, but trust me on this one. And congratulations on the new contract with Brazil. I know that was a tough process. Great work."

Viktor smiled, knowing John's gentlemanly way of closing an argument and ending on a positive note.

"O.K., Frank. Thanks a lot." John said as he hung up.

"Let me guess. Bogus lawsuit." Viktor said to the mirror as he met John's eyes.

"You know it. Getting to be a good way to make a living for a lot of guys."

Viktor couldn't resist. "You know, there was a time when lawyers actually did good things. They were really more like arbitrators, or provided a record of events when needed. Now, I sometimes think they run the country. Everybody sues everybody, usually at the suggestion of an enterprising lawyer. Another reason I don't watch much T.V. Never seen so many lawyer commercials in my life. It's like they encourage you to sue somebody or something. Remember when their governing body wouldn't even let them advertise on T.V.? Said it was not ethical. Guess it became ethical or they lost their ethics." He shook his head. "They're worse than politicians." He laughed. "Wait a minute, they are most politicians."

John laughed, trying to remember how many times he had listened to Viktor's dissertation's about how lawyers were the single biggest reason for the screwed up nature of things. He agreed for the most part, but unfortunately, he employed dozens because you simply couldn't do business anymore without them; a condition they basically created.

John said, "Let's go to Bobby Van's for lunch before we go to the house."

They parked on Main Street in Bridgehampton and sat at a table by the street.

"John, are you going to have any press people at the party?"

"No, they usually get in the way and sometimes piss people off; particularly when they later embellish or distort what went on or what was said."

"What about your friend Pamela Warrick from People Magazine? She has a great reputation for fairness, and many of your friends know and respect her."

"You're right Viktor. It would be fun to have Pamela there. I don't think anyone would be nervous with Pamela's presence. She is very up front and professional. Give her a call, and if she agrees, you can pick her up in the helicopter. Besides, I have a project I'd like to run by her after the meeting."

John greeted an acquaintance passing by the table, then turned back to Viktor.

"Viktor, you know this is going to be the last party like this."

He nodded. As John's only totally trusted confidant, Viktor was very involved with his friends plan and knew they were close to the end.

John continued to speak between eating what he thought was the best steak he ever had.

"I want us to act as normal as we can. I want you to be at the party though I'm aware you don't particularly care for these affairs. Take your last look at the most influential and powerful people in their element and just enjoy it as if it were live theater."

Viktor reluctantly agreed and ate his fish.

"Viktor, have you ever read Frank Feschino's book about the 1952 sightings of UFOs in Braxton County called the *Braxton County Monster*?"

"I have, and it was quite informative. I actually met Frank in a Daytona Beach record store while I was looking to buy a LA Guns record album. Always liked Kelly Nichols as a friend and his amazing ability to play bass guitar. As you probably know, Frank spent over twenty years in the trenches doing research and he is finally getting the respect he deserves."

John agreed and reminded Viktor that all this was about to be made very clear to everyone.

"How about some ice cream at the Candy Kitchen?" John asked as they left Bobby Van's.

"I'm always ready for some of Melinda's wonderful ice cream."

As they strolled leisurely down the sidewalk, John suddenly stopped and faced the street where an endless parade of Bentleys, Rolls Royce's, Porsches, Ferraris, and other high end cars passed by.

"I can remember when Bridgehampton was just a laid back town between Southampton and East Hampton. Most people just drove through, except those who stopped at Bobby Van's." He shook his head.

"Then, Estee Lauder and her son Ronald grabbed a large piece of farm land and built huge estates. Next thing you know, 'McMansions' started popping up all over the place. Bridgehampton was born. Roger Thayer, whose family dates back to the Tories, would tell you it was always here, but even he had to yield to change. He had to build a larger building next to his hardware store which doubled his operating capacity. Things snowballed, and now all the mom and pop stores are gone. Even Sag Harbor, which was so 'unhampton' and wonderful because of that is pretty much a place for the 200 foot yacht folks. Provisions was a hangout for writers and artists, and now it's a grocery store and in that transition, lost its soul. Everything changed. Day trippers dwindled because everything became so expensive that only the rich could afford to be here, even for a visit."

30

Viktor could see that his friend was deeply saddened by the way things had become. "But the ice cream is still great," he said, to lighten the mood.

John laughed. "Yeah, and the biggest scoops in the world. Let's have at it."

They left Candy Kitchen and headed down Montauk Highway. The traffic was starting to build and they agreed it had been a good idea to leave early. As the guard opened the massive gates, Whitmors Nursery was putting the final touches on the special landscaping ordered just for the party, and the massive tent and dance floor were being put into place. A truck from Wines by Morrell was delivering cases of wine and champagne even though John had his own extensive wine cellar.

John loved wine and also had his own private stash at the Twenty-One Club in New York City and the American Hotel in Sag Harbor. His favorite was a '82 Latour or a '61 if he could get one. It was said he had cornered the market for '82 Bordeaux and was very generous with those close friends who also loved wine. He hated wasting wine on those who did not have a developed palette.

The food for his party would be catered by the Palm, known for its steak and lobster. Heavy security had been assembled and parking was a logistical nightmare. It was rumored that the vice president would be there, but only John knew for sure and he wasn't talking.

The party was a great success. When Elton John sang Crocodile Rock, he brought the house down. Viktor amused himself watching all the powerful people around him engaged in economic and political conversation that would be meaningless when John's plan unfolded.

There were plenty of movie stars and the vice president *did* attend. The party was well-planned with special guests who would also meet with John next week in his office. By having the party, he assured they would all be in town and able to make a special meeting. Though most of the men were very rich and powerful in their own right, none would ever decline a meeting invitation from John Klein.

The remainder of the weekend was well-planned. John and Viktor visited with Pat Malloy on his 190 foot yacht *Intuition* and then sailed with him on *Challenge*, his 38 foot Hinckley. The sail was perfect. As it turned out, Viktor knew Pat Malloy quite well. They had organized a sailboat race, the Sag Harbor Cup, in 1983 to raise money to combat drug abuse. After the race, Pat had invited Viktor to race with him around Long Island and numerous races in Florida over the years. The Hinckley was very familiar to him so he took the helm while Pat and John had various discussions.

From there, they went to *Charmed*, a 210 foot yacht custom-built by Benetti that took three years to build. It had everything, including a helicopter and car, as well as many water toys. A planned meeting was held with the vice president while underway in Gardiner's Bay, with a stop at Block Island. Though the vice president would be attending his July 9th meeting, John wanted to feel him out about what the other invited attendees were thinking regarding the big get together. As John knew would be the case, the savvy politician had spoken with several of the other players, and as John had hoped, it appeared no one had any idea why he was calling them together. It was what John had hoped. Everything was going as planned and to those who did not know what was coming, it all seemed quite normal.

CHAPTER FIVE

THE MEETING

July ninth was a beautiful day. The sky was pale blue and the slight west wind made the 81 degree temperature perfect for John's meeting.

A large tent had been erected on top of his office building where the meeting was to be held. No expense was spared. The tent was air-conditioned and the 21 Club would cater the affair which included his own '82 Latour, Lafeete, and Patrous wines. A helicopter lowered the conference table and overstuffed leather chairs to the event work crew. The tent had skylights to maximize light and visibility. Seeing the sky was very important to the meeting. In all four corners of the tent large monitors seemed a bit oversized but very necessary for the presentation. The monitors connected to banks of very sophisticated computers and audio systems. Engineers sat at consoles ready to take commands from John.

The guests started to arrive around 11:30 a.m.. Some came early to get a word in with John before the meeting. It was the top of the "A" list, right out of Forbes richest and most influential people. There were some that no one recognized but all knew by reputation. Like John, these were the movers and shakers of the world who shunned publicity and kept their life a secret. It has often been said that ten people run the world and none of us know who they are. They were present today.

Invitees attended meetings called by John. It did not matter whether you were a Republican or Democrat. He contributed to both parties.

The meeting started off slowly with those in attendance introducing themselves. Some used titles, but most needed no introduction because their names were well known. True to form, those who guarded their identity passed on the introductions. John chuckled because he knew that shortly it would not matter anyway.

Viktor took his customary seat right behind John. He never missed a meeting, even when John met individually with anyone. This made some people uncomfortable, but John felt it also kept them honest.

After introductions, lunch of baby quail in a lemon reduction sauce with asparagus and roasted red potatoes was served. An aged porterhouse steak, roasted red peppers tossed in garlic and angel hair completed the menu.

Once lunch was finished, John thanked the vice president for attending the meeting. He really didn't have a choice because if he wanted to run for president, John could make it happen. Per their unspoken agreement, their earlier meeting was not mentioned.

John started fast, explaining the condition of the world as he and many experts saw it. No one doubted that John had done his homework because they had never heard of an investment he made that didn't turn out well. He had offices all over the world and a staff of more than two hundred researchers constantly feeding him data. Many believed he had a sixth sense when it came to predicting trends, and almost certainly he had inherited Sirta's ESP.

John told the gathering that the world was in grave danger. The environment and the economy were both in major trouble. He stated that he did not feel the sins of the past could be reversed and the situation well past the point of being fixed. He spoke of dramatic climate change, citing Hurricane Sandy and the increase of tornadoes and tsunami flooding as prime examples.

Having gotten everyone's attention, John continued. "The middle class is vanishing, moving to join the ranks of the poor in astronomical numbers around the world. Famine is widespread and water is becoming scarce. New types of diseases are popping up all over the world with mutant strains so strong that none of our drugs today can cure them. GMO is killing the planet and its people, and this is but a small part of the food chain that is contaminated. Meat, especially beef and chicken, is being manipulated and more and more people are getting cancer and other diseases as a result."

John took a sip of water and continued. "The world economy is on the verge of collapsing. Multi-trillions of dollars are owed by citizens, banks, and governments. The real story about how much the world banking system owes has never been told. The euro has been in trouble for years, and there isn't enough money in Germany to save it. Germany and her largest trading partner, China, will collapse as China slows down. This will also happen to Australia, Canada, and New Zealand because they are all heavily dependent on China.

"Every country is bankrupt and no one wants to make the sacrifices required to save it. Even if they did, it's too late to save the euro. In America, the Federal Reserve is printing $85 billion a month to keep the economy going. The dollar is being diluted and to pay our bills, our government will have to devalue the dollar. When they do, everyone's wealth will be cut in half.

" Hyperinflation is on the way and having gold and silver will not matter. Many cities in America are bankrupt. The burden of pension funds has buried them in debt, along with years of irresponsible spending. The Chinese are in a bubble and can only survive if the world is healthy and does not slow down. They are loaded with US dollars and getting very nervous about it. They have started to dump their dollars by buying up companies all around the world. They are afraid to get rid of their dollars in other ways because it may cause the dollar to collapse and that would cost them even more money. They are bartering more and more to get away from the dollar and would love to see the dollar not connected to oil. In fact, when oil is not pegged to the dollar, it will fall. This can happen at any time because the process has started."

John paused and looked around the room. "I have brought you all together today because I believe only a very radical solution is going to save the world. Human nature, as we have recently seen in Greece, is not to give back any benefits. It will be no different in any other country. We all know that if you give back too much, the economy will collapse. There is no formula to save us. If we spend, we are in trouble, if we don't we are in trouble. Some of you may think the solution is a One World Currency. In fact, I know some of you around this table are positioning yourself for just that move."

He glanced knowingly at a few people.

"You think you will be the new leaders and dictators of the world. Those who do fail to understand human nature. History repeats itself and you will tumble just like those who came before you. Yes, we all unfortunately understand how lazy and complacent most humans are, but when you push them to the wall they come alive, and here in America there are more citizens with guns than ever before. The government just said they will not stop the sale of assault weapons, and I recently found out they ordered the largest quantity of ammunition in history. This raises the question 'what is the government getting prepared for?'"

The vice president shifted in his chair as John continued.

"Now, more than ever, the world will not accept a one-world currency. Your plans will be exposed over the Internet and the Occupy Wall Street movement will rise again. This time it may not be so peaceful. The people will be armed and they will go after you. The military will not help you, and you could never pay an army big enough to stop the masses. Riots will break out all over the world, governments will tumble, and those responsible will be dealt with in the most harsh manner imaginable. You don't have to look back very far in history for an example. The Russian people executed Czar Nickolas and his entire family for failing to understand human nature. You all can cite examples of what happens when you push people too far. The world will not accept a one-world currency from those who took them down in the first place. Never underestimate what people will do, and now armed with the internet and guns, they are more powerful than ever before."

Again John took a long sip of water and tried to read the audience. "Sorry to be painting such a dark picture today, but I know how all of you think. It's why I brought you together today. We all tend to think the world is how we see it and live it. Our little circle of friends in our little neighborhood is the world. I am sure the vice president has never met several of the ladies and gentlemen sitting at this table. Never even knew they existed, but at the same time wondered how certain things got done in the world."

He looked directly at the vice president.

"You've been in government for quite some time and thought the Carlyle Group was powerful. In a way they are, but they all have egos, and that is why they are out front. Some of the visibility is unavoidable since being a past US president or prime minister of England makes one quite recognizable. By no means do I want to take away from their power and influence. The point is, they are puppets, along with Goldman Sachs., J.P. Morgan, Bank of America, etc.

" Those who rule the world are unknown and they want more power than ever before. The human race, all of us, have never understood that sharing the wealth and power makes us all more powerful. Just look at how many years we tried to hold women down and it still goes on to some degree but not like it did just a hundred years ago. We finally let them vote and hold high paying jobs and the world has benefited greatly by it. The same can be said of the black man. Yet still in this country and around the world, discrimination goes on. Religion is still the focus of many wars. How many people have died in the name of God?"

John glanced up as a low-flying helicopter went overhead. "Our DNA has been so corrupted over the centuries that human nature has evolved far from what was intended, and I cannot see how we can ever come back. I know for a fact that all of you are preparing for the worst. Many have bought small islands and fortified them. Yes, you can do farming on them and you have bought tons of seed. You can grow your own cattle and fish. The mistake you make is believing you can insulate yourself from the wrath that will come down on every person here when those we discounted find us. And they will find us."

John paused for effect and prepared to shift gears.

"How many of you have contemplated just how vast the universe is?" He paused and sipped water. "Over the years I have spent a great deal of time and money exploring the universe. Those of you who know me well know I have backed a number of space exploration projects, and have financially supported several satellite projects. The government has not been honest about UFOs. After talking to many experts, I do believe this planet has been visited, and I know for a fact there is intelligent life on other planets. I will explain how I know that later."

There were several glances exchanged. " I see no end to the universe because for me, the ending is always the beginning of something else. So how can there be an end? The fact that we are here means we have always been here. Newton said that energy can neither be created nor destroyed. So what some call the *soul* might also be called energy."

Some in the audience began murmuring and shuffling in place.

"Please, bear with me a few moments more." The voices around the table quieted. "Organized religion put a twist on science and enlightened beings as a way to get power and control the masses. Books have recently come out that enable the ordinary citizen to understand the science of quantum physics. Positive thinking as a way of life was

39

explained in Napoleon Hill's book, *Think and Grow Rich* many years ago and is still being quoted today. The point is that more and more we are seeing a blending of science and religion. Latest statistics show that people are moving away from organized religion. Living 'in the now' is the new mantra. The past is gone. We don't know anything about the future, so living in the *now*, the present moment, is the only place to be. Much on this subject is being written and talked about by noted authors like Eckardt Tolle. His books and DVDs are sold worldwide. His lectures are always sold out. People are getting it.

" Living in the now will bring you the most peace and happiness. This new movement is catching on and getting the attention of a very large audience. If you look carefully, Joe Campbell was right, all religions are telling the same story and putting their own twist on it. The masses are fed up, and they're looking for alternatives.

"The best book I have ever read was authored by Michael A. Singer. *The Untethered Soul,* written in 2007, was on the New York Times bestseller list for months. The author is related to Michael Singer who invented the Singer sewing machine. He lives on 600 acres in Florida. While working on his PhD, Singer decided to go on a spiritual path. He could have done anything with his life and instead he chose enlightenment. He made it easy to read and understand how best to be in the now. The important point is that his book and others like it are showing the way to a more peaceful and happy life, and the popularity of those books show that people are listening.

"Blending the thinking of some of the best and most revered minds in the world is becoming the *new* way to be, so to speak. This is the future and it is here now. Everything *is*. We are all part of the universe, all connected in some way. This is the way it has always been and this is the way it will remain forever."

He smiled and his tone became less formal. "I realize I've put many things in your head to think about, so let's take a short break and go into it further when the break is over."

During the break all the participants were asking each other what was the point of all of this. They knew most, if not all the information already; a fact John was well aware of. On the sidelines, John listened but was not surprised by the reaction from the group. He intended to go on anyway because by the time the meeting ended, the points he was about to make would be clear.

The facts and figures John presented after the recess surprised many of the attendees. Most knew how bad it was, but didn't realize how out of control it all was. They took another short break, and this time the conversation was more sober and many clung to every word John said. This was part of his plan because he knew what came next required their full attention. After all, he wanted this group to invest billions of dollars in what he believed was the solution to the world's problems.

This would be a tough group to convince and all his information had to be spot on, with factual research to back it up. This was the biggest project of his lifetime and it was imperative that he convinced them how serious he was, and more importantly, that he knew exactly what he was doing.

The break ended. Pellegrino replaced wine immediately after lunch because he needed everyone's full attention. The fate of the world hung on what was accomplished here today.

John spent the next several minutes talking about his love of outer space and why he had invested so much time, money, and energy into discovering as much as possible. His aim was to convince them that science was more than just a hobby, and show why he used it in every aspect of his life with great rewards. The study of space had a great significance to him, and he needed to convince them that space held the answers to the world's problems.

He stated very clearly that he knew as a fact there was life on other planets, and there were other solar systems like ours in infinite space.

With that said, and while the murmuring subsided, he asked Viktor to explain some of the fine points of his plan. What their reactions would be was anybody's guess.

John sat back and contemplated how he had gotten all this accomplished. For the first time in five years, he allowed himself to think about all that had happened.

So much had transpired over years filled with great memories as well as disappointments. The project he had almost abandoned was now his crowning achievement but more important, it would transform a decaying earth.

PART II

THE BEGINNING

CHAPTER SIX

BUILDING THE ANTENNA

John knew he needed a very secure and secret place, so he bought an island in the South Pacific which had never been inhabited. The end goal was to build a massive antenna system designed to communicate with other life forms. He calculated the entire project would take at least five years. He was aware that his project might be photographed by satellites, and he wanted it to be a total secret until he was ready to tell the world about it. The goal was to be able to present indisputable truth so political and religious establishments could not dispute it. He knew how powerful they were in suppressing information about UFO's and he was not going to let that happen.

He chose a very remote island with a deep harbor capable of accommodating seaplanes to fly supplies in or out. To move larger equipment and material without creating suspicion he had a custom yacht built by Palmer Johnson that was three-hundred seven feet in length. He instructed them to only do the hull and superstructure and his team of engineers would do the finishing. They had built boats for him before so they didn't argue. Basically, the interior of the ship was wide open and the exterior looked like a personal yacht. To ensure secrecy, he instructed his engineers to design the antenna in modules that would not only fit in the yacht but looked like they were being manufactured as part of it. In this way he could bring in supplies undetected by air or sea.

The unloading dock was a building with a large overhang roof. The yacht would be backed up to the dock and large anchors would be used to keep it steady. Everything was unloaded off the stern of the boat through large doors that John told Palmer Johnson he needed to drive a car in and out. Not an unusual request because they had already created spaces over the years in the sterns of other yachts for all sorts of water toys and affixed doors to them.

Because this yacht was over three-hundred feet, it would have a beam large enough as it went aft to easily have a full-size garage door on it. This was not your typical garage door because it would be operated by hydraulics and was watertight. When the yacht was backed into place it was impossible to see what was being unloaded or reloaded. The dock was fixed with conveyor belts that immediately sent the cargo underground to the assembly complex.

He had a number of dwellings built strategically to surround the harbor. The rest of the island was mountainous and not very habitable. The only way on and off the island was by boat, and the only landing possible was in the harbor. The rest of the island dropped straight into the sea. It was an old extinct volcano which made it perfect for what John had in mind.

He had a modest manor house built for himself. The rest of the dwellings housed the scientists, engineers, and workers. It had the appearance of a private resort, and there were plenty of No Trespassing signs.

A full-time security detail circled the island in speedboats, and there was an elaborate video surveillance system. Every inch of the island was under constant surveillance.

His workers committed to a five-year contract. He paid them one million dollars a year with a five million dollar bonus promised at the end. They were all made to sign confidentiality agreements and could have no communication with the outside world. The scientists and engineers were paid double. Once they set foot on the island they could not leave for five years, and it was easy with that pay to get many qualified personnel.

John did all he could to make it as comfortable as possible, but he also knew they would be very busy because what he was going to attempt would take a lot of work and concentration.

His plan was simple to state, not so simple to implement; to build the most advanced antenna ever attempted in the world. His goal was to communicate with another planet deep in space. Money was no object since he had more than he could ever spend and just kept making money on top of that money. He gave no thought to making his mark in history. The objective was to change the world for future generations, but the unexpected happened.

It took three years to build the antenna. During that time a number of computers became outdated. New ones were quickly put into place. He knew there were other antennas around the world trying to communicate with outer space and he had gotten regular updates about their equipment and progress. Since they weren't being successful, he and his scientists knew they needed to do something very radical. They knew they needed a different type of antenna; one that was beyond the power of anything in existence today. It would need a sustainable power source, so they built their own nuclear power plant. This not only powered up the antenna but also supplied the entire island with power.

Because of the island's location, steel would not make sense for the antenna, so his engineers invented a combination of titanium, platinum, and gold wrapped in carbon fiber. All cables used were two-inch solid gold with solid gold connectors. Engineers tweaked a tube Harman/Kardon amplifier connected to B&W horn speakers custom-made to their specs. Each pair were positioned in a specially designed sound room and then hardwired to Macintosh CD recorders, backed up by three-inch Alpha tape recorders. This was being built while the antenna was assembled and updated as new technology became available.

John loved music, so many an afternoon he could be found in music Nirvana or "ear candy heaven" as he called it. He brought a hard drive containing over four thousand albums with him, none of which were compressed and just plugged it into the optical port on the tube preamp.

Assembly of the antenna had proved to be difficult because new ways of soldering titanium, platinum, and gold had to be invented. This required a three-stage process because first the parts being put together had to be heated until they were blood red, then the three-part solder had to be applied at the molting state and all cooled within moments of application. Once perfected, a signal would pass through perfectly at light speed. The signal had to be pure, with absolutely no outside interference or noise. For that reason, no other system in the complex shared any of the power or connectors of the antenna. All switches and connectors were solid gold.

The cone at the top of the antenna was shaped like two Angels facing each other with wings and arms outstretched and bent backwards. At the base, extra windings of gold wire were laced and then threaded to the top, intersecting the Angels at every point. This truly was a sight to behold. As the gold wire reflected the sun' rays, light waves seemed to emanate from the angels. The rest of the antenna looked like standard commercial construction with straight lines connected by supports and anchored into the ground.

The men and women who worked on the project were all artisans and their weld points and connections were always perfect. This was critical because the antenna had to be perfect, with no spaces or gaps. This would ensure any signal picked up would be relayed perfectly through the gold cables to the receiver. The area was always kept immaculately clean.

The manner in which the outside work was performed made it almost impossible to tell it was a construction area. Everyone on the team could do any number of tasks and did so on a regular basis. They had to do more than just build the antenna because an infrastructure had to be built to support everyday living and the entire complex.

Once a month, the yacht would bring supplies. This included new movies that turned out to be the number one source of entertainment on the island. Workers would participate in water sports from time to time, and fishing was one of the favorites. This not only proved to be fun but also supplied the group with fresh fish. The cook was not gourmet, yet he turned out amazing meals enjoyed by all. It was not easy being away from loved ones with no communication for such a long period of time. This was all calculated by John and he hired just the right number of people so they would always be busy, but not too busy. This kept their mind on the work and that proved to be therapeutic.

John had hired a team of psychologists early on to consult during the team recruiting process to help ensure only those who could adjust to an extended absence lifestyle were hired. Viktor suggested that they also hire four of the psychologists to stay for the project duration. This proved invaluable as they monitored and, when necessary, intervened to assist those few who showed signs of stress, or in two cases, requested to be released from their commitment and leave. In each instance, counseling and minor adjustments resolved the situations and no one ever left the project.

Finally, everything was done. The antenna was set deep in the ground with the top camouflaged by clamshells. When opened, it would be exposed to the atmosphere. John decided to turn it on only at night so it could not be photographed by satellites and planes. This was later changed to an all-day schedule once they figured out how to better camouflage it. John, who was not happy with all the down time, forced this issue.

They deduced that it really didn't matter what was in front of the antenna as long as it was not solid. While developing a solution, they actually came up with a better antenna.

John remembered his first FM stereo antenna, which was nothing more than a speaker wire connected to the back of the receiver and run up the wall, where it would split. This was also true of cars when antennas were removed from the bodywork and a wire was put into the windshield. John realized they may have stumbled on why all other antennas had failed to communicate with other planets.

It had to do with their size and construction. So why not make the entire island an antenna? To do this, his engineers started running quarter-inch copper mixed with strands of gold and silver from the head of the antenna all across the island. They put lead grounding plates on the ends and placed them in the water. John's thought was that maybe they could even use the ocean as part of the antenna system.

All the wire was painted dark green and covered when possible. The antenna itself was camouflaged by creating artificial trees and bushes and arranging them on a chicken wire like maze suspended above the antenna, then curved gently to make it look like it was part of the landscape. When John saw the wires used to suspend the chicken wire he came up with the idea of expanding the antenna. The idea was discussed at length among the scientists, and they all agreed it would work and make it a much better receiver and transceiver. It would take eighteen months, but all agreed it would be worth it in the end. In the meantime, they could use the antenna the way it was.

On July 7, 2007, John threw the switch. Everything came online as it should. It took a tremendous amount of power to get all the systems going, but they had it.

First, the banks of computers started lighting up like the Christmas tree in Rockefeller Center, followed by receivers, transverse, and recording devices. John put on a set of newly designed headphones that looked more like a space helmet. The idea was to keep all outside noise completely out and only let in whatever the antenna was picking up. There were three stations manned twenty-four hours a day in three-hour shifts. Operators were not allowed to do anything else during that period of time but listen.

About a month into the listening, Viktor was at the console and thought he heard something. The level of excitement was so high you could cut through it with a knife. The sound engineers took about three hours to determine it wasn't anything significant, but they knew the system was working because it had received something, whatever it was. During this time the extra antenna wires were being laid and hopes were high that they would help.

Month after month went by with nothing. John decided the cable should have branches because this would give even more surface area to the antenna. Every hundred yards the wire was grounded. He believed this enhanced the ability to source the entire island as an antenna. Finally all the wires were in place and the grounding plates with their very heavy lead ends placed in the ocean.

While all this was going on, the engineers were working on how to power up such a large grid. It was decided mini solar power stations had to be built, and they could not be noticeable from the air. A new solar panel had to be invented that did not reflect the sun and had maximum absorption of its rays. Special alloys were developed and manufactured on site. Never before was the sun's power harnessed so efficiently in such a small package.

Science was taking big leaps and John knew it. He felt none of this would be in vain and just kept pouring more money into the project. Whatever his engineers and scientists asked for, they got. Nothing was going to stop his quest to communicate with the outside world.

CHAPTER SEVEN

THE COMMUNICATION

Finally everything was in place. The island was crisscrossed with cables and many power stations. The computers were upgraded along with the receivers and the transceivers. The engineers modified Classe equipment with their own electronics so that in the end not much was left but the original shell.

Still, days went by with no results. Morale was getting low, and some were even talking about going home. John reminded them that they were in for a five-year commitment and he had invested most of his fortune in the project so everyone was going to see it through. The team of psychologists were having their professional skills put to the ultimate test.

John was spending the majority of his time on the island interacting with team members, trying in every way possible to keep morale up. He and Viktor dreamed up a variety of organized activities designed to keep everyone involved and active. He even had his engineers start other unrelated projects which not only caused a more productive atmosphere but also yielded positive results in many cases.

While he knew that failure was always a possibility, it was something he didn't like to think about, though he did have a plan for that.

If, at the end of five years there were no results, he would turn the project over to the government, and they could take it from there. He hadn't wanted the government involved because he was very familiar with the red tape and bureaucratic nonsense that would destroy a great idea. He also knew they would not be honest if they ever heard anything. He thought they may have already heard something and were not telling the public because of the religious lobby.

Some believed that if the world did not have religion, it would fall into chaos. This was fostered by very well-placed religious leaders and lobbyists. John knew better and had rejected organized religion long ago. He knew that if people lived in the moment, in the *now*, they wouldn't need organized religion, so he was determined to keep the government out of the project and go it on his own. John had learned a lot from his wife, and it had changed his life. He always believed in positive thinking but never understood until recently how to harness the positive energy of the universe on a regular basis. This project was not going to fail, and what was most important he believed it.

At 3 a.m. on October 10, 2010, John Rogers, John's most trusted scientist on the project, heard something. A few minutes later he heard it again. This time it was even clearer than the first time. A distinct "hello" was recorded.

He hit the alarm button, signaling the other engineers that something was heard. Most were in bed but got up immediately and went to the sound laboratory. Tapes were confirmed; they had heard the word "hello." The lab started broadcasting, "Hello, do you hear us?" every five seconds. Finally, a response came back.

"Is this the planet Earth?"

Excitement grew because they knew for sure that this wasn't a communication from within the solar system or the space station.

Rogers replied, "Yes, this is Earth. Where are you?"

There was a long silence and then the reply came. "We are many light-years away in a far corner many universes away from you. We are calculating just how far away we are. We attempted to communicate with you several times but only now have been able to reach you. Your signal was clear, but you were obviously not able to hear ours until now. The size of your antenna has made the difference. It appears you have been able to harness the entire earth and all its minerals as one large antenna."

Rogers quickly turned to the other scientists and said, " grounding the antenna in the ocean, coupled with all the power stations we connected made all the silver, gold, copper, and plutonium on the planet a part of our antenna system."

While this was going on, John was off the island attending to finances because the project was always in need of more money. A code had been established when communicating to keep the project secret. Now, as they told him the fishing was the best ever, and he might want to find time to come to the island, he knew something big had happened.

John immediately called Viktor and told him to make arrangements to get them to the island as soon as possible. This meant taking the helicopter which Viktor piloted. It was custom-built by Northrop Grumman with extra large fuel tanks that required only two stops for fuel. It had every amenity and the newest electronic gizmos and basically flew itself. A helipad had been built on top of the manor house so that access and egress was always easy.

John was anxious, but tried not to let himself get too excited yet. He only had cryptic information and didn't want to get consumed with joy only to be let down later. In his gut, he felt they had had a breakthrough. He asked Viktor what he thought.

"Well John, I think you are about to make history. Your idea to wire the entire island and ground it into the sea has paid off. You are on the verge of taking the world in an entirely new direction. This is even bigger than Christopher Columbus. The ramifications are too big for me to get my mind around. You managed to keep the project a secret and keep the government out of it. You are the visionary, businessman, and inventor the world needed, and I am so proud to know you and be with you throughout this project."

John knew Viktor wasn't kissing ass because he didn't need to and never had.

"Thanks Viktor, that really means a lot to me. Most might have thought I was nuts to embark on this project, but you encouraged me all the way. So many times, when we want to try something new, others try to talk us out of it, but you never did that. This is a five year commitment and we will see it through, whatever the outcome. You being by my side all the way has been important. It's hard for me to truly express myself at this time, but I believe you're right, the world is about to change. 'Everything Is' will become the new mantra the world will follow. This understanding will have profound ramifications on all segments of society and the environment. When people understand that what they do to all that surrounds them directly affects them, they will change. My hope is that a much more advanced planet will be able to teach us what they have learned. Maybe then, we can save ours."

Viktor studied his friend. "I sure hope this is what we've been waiting for, but it could turn out to be just another noise they haven't heard before."

John knew what his trusted confidant was doing. He laughed. "Okay, my friend, I promise I won't cry if it turns out to be nothing."

"Well, you know what I mean." Viktor responded.

"I do, and I appreciate your concern." He glanced out at the churning ocean below them and turned back to Viktor. "This is it, Viktor. I feel it. I can't explain it, but I know." He sat back in his seat and closed his eyes, a knowing smile on his face.

CHAPTER EIGHT

CONTACT

The helicopter landed on the manor house without incident. The house had been built on the leeward corner of the cove, protected from the ocean wind so that the helicopter could always be landed in any kind of weather. It was the only landing site on the rugged island.

John got out and ran to the laboratory while scientists briefed him on what had happened. Viktor had never seen him run so fast and cautioned him to slow down. The path was uneven with many rough spots. But there was no talking to him as he sprinted to the laboratory.

Once inside, he was greeted with cheers and applause. He had done it, and everyone was excited for him and themselves. He stopped briefly to talk to them even though he was desperate to get the latest info. They deserved a few words. Thanking them for their dedication and hard work, he told them their sacrifices were about to change the world for all time, and they all would go down in history. This was a moment in time for all time. There was loud cheering.

Finally, he was able to get to the lead scientist for the latest information. As it turned out, "Planet X" as they called it, only wanted to talk to John, and they had asked for him by name.

"They were very polite, but had no interest in talking to us," his lead engineer said. "So we have been put on hold since we made the first contact."

John asked if they were sure we were in contact with another planet and not just someone who'd hacked into the system. They told him the information they had so far all led to a much higher intelligence than we have on Earth, and they were sure it was another planet.

John was overcome with a sense of relief. He had done it. Hundreds of millions of dollars invested, with no help from the government, he had accomplished the single most significant event in the world's history, and he knew nothing would ever be the same for him or the planet.

He took a seat at the console and spoke into the mike. "Hello from Planet Earth. This is John Klein."

After the few moments it took for his voice to travel millions of miles into space, a reply came back.

"We have been eager to talk to you for a very long time. This is Jebumo from the planet Plytar. It is very good to finally talk to you, John Klein. We have been waiting for you for many of your Earth years."

John replied, "And we have been waiting for you for a very long time."

Jebumo replied, "We have been trying for years to contact Earth, but your antennas were not powerful enough to receive us. Now it looks like the entire Earth is one big antenna, making contact possible."

John asked, "Where are you?"

"Between you and us are many other galaxies very similar to ours that have life on them. Some are more developed than others. All seem to go through the same development stages and eventually either destroy their planets or evolve into a blissful existence. Somehow over the many centuries, the DNA of humans has become corrupted. It wasn't always this way. It evolved. There was a time when humans lived in bliss and harmony. That was before greed took hold. When greed became a strong force it led to aggression and war. Power became an obsession, along with endless desires. Before this, everyone was equal and no one ate the flesh of any other living thing. Plants have all the nourishment required and they have always been plentiful. As it turns out, you need much less good land to feed the beings on the planet if they eat vegetables. Much more is required to raise and slaughter animals for consumption."

There was a brief static interruption, then Jebumo continued. "When or where DNA was mutated, I am not sure. It is very possible there was a race that spread it to other planets. What I do know is that it needs to be stopped. Your planet is on the verge of economic and environmental collapse. If you don't act soon, there will be no Earth as you know it today."

"What exactly do you mean?" John heard himself saying.

" It is possible, and I've seen this before, that your planet will self-destruct. Right now you have global warming dictating your weather and your leaders are not doing enough about it. This will accelerate as your industrial countries continue to build factories that emit pollution that is killing your atmosphere. As this continues and water becomes more scarce, small wars will break out between states in countries as well as countries with other countries. You're already seeing runaway diseases that cannot be stopped by your modern medicine. More and more people are dying of cancer and you don't have to look further than the epidemic in skin cancer to know the sun is not being filtered properly.

"As I said before, I have seen this on other planets. Unfortunately, I was not able to reach many in time, and now they are vast wastelands so polluted that no life forms exist. In the end, their governments fell apart because they could not solve their problems, and civil war broke out as people fought over food and water. No corner of their world was safe as millions fled to whoever they thought might save them. The very rich and priviledged were the first to be hit. Armed gangs easily overwhelmed their security forces. No one was safe and in the end, atomic weapons were used. The planets were destroyed."

John listened in stunned silence as Jebumo continued. "Your planet is heading in this direction. I fear you don't have much time left before it happens, so you must act quickly."

John replied, "I know we have problems, and I know they are bad, but we've been able to solve our problems over the centuries and I believe we will still be able to."

Jebumo replied, "John Klein, you are a smart man, but you are too close to the problem—at the same time, far away. To those in your circle, everything is fine, but they don't spend enough time out of the circle. The poor are poorer than they have ever been and the middle class is becoming poor. People like you are getting richer and you add to your ranks every year. Where is all this money coming from? The poor will be complacent for only so long and then uprisings will start. Your elusive dollar is being weakened for a reason and when it is no longer the currency recognized by the world, so goes America. Is America too big to fail? Is the Euro too big to fail? Who will be able to save them both? China is in a bubble and it will burst when the Dollar and Euro fail. They will, because there isn't enough money in your world to save them. You know this. We are not talking years; we are talking months or tomorrow. So something has to be done *now*."

Those in the room looked at each other. How could beings on another planet be so familiar with earth's systems?

As if reading their thoughts, Jebumo replied, "Yes, we are familiar with your processes, and we have seen them, in various forms, before.

"Some on your planet have been planning total domination for quite some time because greed is the worst sickness you humans have," Jebumo said. "They want One World Currency so they can be the new kings of the world. This will work for a while because the people will go with anyone who will feed them.

"There will no longer be any form of democracy; there will be the super rich and the workers. After a while, human nature will take over as it always does, and worldwide revolution will take place with the military siding with the people. After all, they are people too and their families are hungry and slaves in the New World order. We believe you are the best person on your planet for us to talk to."

"How do you know all this? You understand our currency system?" John interjected again.

"We know, as you will soon discover, and yes, we understand your system. This is not new and I can tell you it

61

does not work. I would like you to try to imagine how big the universe is and then to imagine the universe next to yours and then the universe next to that and so forth and so on. Hard to imagine infinite space. The ending of one is the beginning of another. Build a wall and make it as thick as you want, but there will always be two sides. So now think of the infinite possibilities of other planets just like yours. Once you do this, you'll realize how many infinite times your experience has happened on other planets. You have not seen it yet, but I have and they all go down because of greed. The only way to survive is to share everything. This ends aggression. There is no need to worry about whether or not someone is contributing or just living off of others. Why? Because no one cares when everyone needs so much less, and no one is looking for power, so contentment sets in. Why don't you live with bliss right now?"

There was silence until John realized Jebumo was waiting for him to answer. "Well, I don't know…I suppose there are lots of reasons." John managed to reply, though he had the feeling his answer was not required.

"Your world has been at war ever since you started to eat meat. Was this evolution? I don't think so. I believe you were visited by another planet with beings like yourself who had to flee their dying planet and unfortunately they spread their DNA to your population. I have seen too many planets evolve without greed. Their beings evolved and their environment stayed intact. They invented supercomputers and figured out how to sustain life. They were able to retrieve their dead and bring them back to life again. They all coexist today in bliss. Some of you might call it heaven. I call your Earth hell. Who is happy on Earth?

"You start your life taking one of your last breaths. You know your entire life you will die one day and your life is never complete. The shadow of death surrounds you and you never know the meaning of life. You get old and your body falls apart, slows down. Your golden years are tarnished and you have no way of getting rid of the tarnish. Yet today, your science could evolve with stem cell research, but it is slowed down by your politicians and religious fanatics. The point is, you are close, but time is running out. Your planet could go one of two ways but I fear it is too set in stone right now to ever right itself. Something dramatic has to happen."

John was dumbfounded. He knew things were bad but didn't realize just how bad. He thought of the Jews in Germany as Hitler was taking over. How some of them just refused to believe it could happen to them. The smart ones left, but millions stayed behind.

This is what is going on in the world right now, he thought, and it was happening to him, the richest man in the world. He knew that all his money was not going to save him, his family, or earth, and he had to do something.

"What am I supposed to do?" He asked Jebumo.

"Everything happens for a reason and everything you have done to this point was supposed to happen. The fact that we are talking today is linked to every single thing you have done in your life to this point. You have in your power the means to change the planet forever."

John asked, "Why do you want to save the Earth?"

Jebumo explained, "The universes have been plagued by the bad strain of DNA as far back as anyone can remember. How it mutated no one knows and it took several millions of years to come up with a solution. On your planet, your religious people call it heaven and hell. These words are really talking about energy being negative—hell—or positive—heaven. Some say you can't have a positive without a negative. This is the thinking on your planet. I can tell you that you can have only positive because I live it every day. Would you then say I live in heaven? If that is what you want to call it, that's fine. I am in the bliss of eternal positive energy. Negative energy can be eliminated from your life.

" This should be easy for you to see as such a successful man. You must have had to think positive all of your life to get this far. I am sure along the way you met negative people and noticed that all they do is complain and are sick most of the time. Well, they've surrounded themselves with negative energy. This negative energy attracts more negative energy and this then becomes their life. The story they live by. How many times have you heard these people say, 'it's just my luck'? This then becomes their life, and it is their hell. The point is, we need to eliminate negative energy from your planet by changing your DNA. I have taken it upon myself, along with others of my kind to rid the universes of this DNA. It is taking many years, but you and I talking today is proof it is working. Before earth implodes, I would like to show you the way to bliss."

There was a brief silence, and Jebumo added, "Why do we want to save your world? Because, at the moment, Earth, and those who inhabit it are worth saving. That is why."

CHAPTER NINE
THE CHAMBER

After speaking with Jebumo for several minutes, John's head was reeling and he was tired. The trip had also taken a lot out of him. Because this decision was so important, he suggested they talk after he had rested. Jebumo agreed and advised John that they now could communicate at anytime.

John went back to the manor house with Viktor, but his pace was much different this time. So much was swirling in his head, he felt he would not be able to sleep, but once his head hit the pillow, he was fast asleep. When Viktor woke him several hours later as instructed, he sat up, feeling dazed. He looked at his friend.

"Viktor, I had the most amazing dream. A bright light was shining over my head. It seemed to penetrate right through my body. I felt I was one with everything and everything I saw was connected to everything else."

John rubbed his eyes and continued. "I was suspended in bliss and just kept attracting more bliss wherever I traveled. I saw bliss in everything, and whenever negative thoughts would try to creep in, positive energy would hold them back. I could see and read the auras of everything from rocks to animals because they all give off some form of energy. I have never in my life felt so close to being a part of the universe. I decided to try to fly so I arched my back, started to run, and before I knew it, I was in the air. At first, flying above everyone made me nervous, especially when I saw electric lines. I landed and took off again several times. Before long, I felt I could teach others to fly as I soared over buildings and forms."

He looked at Viktor. "The dream was so real I feel that I could fly right now."

"You think they can fly on Jebumo's planet?" Viktor said.

"Sounds like they can do pretty much what they want to. Hard to imagine that kind of freedom."

Viktor looked thoughtful. "Can you remember the first time your parents let you out of the house by yourself?" Not waiting for an answer, he continued, "You stood there all alone, probably thinking to yourself 'I'm free. I may be only in my backyard, but the next time it'll be across the street'. As your new freedom washes over you, the feeling of being finally untethered sinks in and you feel strength and confidence. Maybe you jump up and down and spin around. Then it occurs to you that soon your friends will be free and you can all jump up and down and explore." He looked reflective for a moment. "Maybe that's what we are about to feel."

John clapped his hands together and laughed. "I like it."

After John finished dressing, he ate a quick breakfast and headed to the laboratory. Once again he was greeted by cheers and applause. Everyone was there and by now had come to understand just how important the project was. John quickly went to the console and put on the earphones.

"Jebumo, are you there?"

Jebumo instantly replied. "I am always here."

"What are we supposed to do next?" John asked.

"We need to meet on my planet so you can see firsthand how advanced we are and how your planet could do the same."

Jebumo then gave John directions on how to build a chamber that would transport him through space, not unlike *Star Trek* beaming people from place to place. The only way John could get to Plytar was to have his body broken down into microscopic particles and reassembled in another time and place. He also asked John to bring Viktor with him because his mind alone might not be able to absorb all that was about to happen, and he would need the verification of another being that everything in fact was happening and true.

John agreed and the process of building the chamber began.

***

The parts to build the chamber had to be ordered and then modified according to the plans given by Jebumo. This was no easy task because many of the metal compounds did not exist and new electronics had to be invented. Space was made in the laboratory for an eight foot by ten foot chamber. New electrical lines had to be dedicated to accept full power from the nuclear generator. All other systems would have to be shut off in order to achieve enough power to send them into space.

The lead walls were six inches thick so nothing inside the chamber could escape. If it did, John or Viktor might lose an ear or an eye or some other part when their bodies were broken down. The walls were covered with mirrors one-inch thick. A small window of six-inch glass was infused into the lead door which closed like a safe. The floor had two three-foot disks designed for them to stand on. The disks rotated slowly as laser beams were shot at them from all angles.

People to be transported wore special titanium souls on their shoes designed to keep them grounded to the disk. The disks would spin slowly, gathering speed until reaching top speed at about 9000 RPMs. If all went well at 9000 RPMs, the subjects would disappear.

Special clothing was designed, that by all appearances, did not look any different than protective clothing used by a motorcycle rider. These however, had threads of Mylar woven with very thin threads of Kevlar, mixed with silver. They were made to be strong enough to accept the energy and be able to break down for transport and then reassembled at the destination end.

No helmet was required or extra oxygen since the atmosphere on Plytar was just like that on earth and the temperature was a constant seventy-five degrees all over the planet.

Completing the work laid out by Jebumo was not without mishap. While the engineers and scientists led by John Rogers worked around the clock, they were tested more than once. They were, after all, building equipment designed to do things that were not even theory or conceptual on earth. As the best in their respective fields, this was on the one hand exciting, but on the other, cause for much argument and debate on the 'how to'. One such very heated argument was underway as John entered one of the labs one morning.

Rogers, in the middle of the argument, held his hand up when John approached.

"Okay, okay, let's take a break, think about it, and re-group in thirty."

As the other men walked away mumbling, Rogers turned to John. "Nerves getting a bit frayed, boss."

"So I see. What's the problem?"

"Well, no problem, really. It's just that we're breaking so much new ground, everyone has their own idea about how to proceed." He laughed and continued. "You've heard that old saying about scientist's being like squirrels. Well, every now and then, these guys run around barking like a bunch of squirrels and don't take time to hear what their fellow squirrel is saying."

"I'd say that's normal. We've both seen it happen on other projects, particularly when work is being done on a project that is so unusual." John said.

"Unusual!" Rogers exclaimed. "My God John, have you thought about what we're doing?"

"Of course I have. It's a whole new arena of science and engineering."

"New! John, it boggles the mind." He shook his head in bewilderment. "this system is supposed to break your body into who knows how many pieces, then transport it to another planet." He paused. "A planet we didn't even know existed." He added.

John had a big grin on his face. "There you have it."

"There you have it." Rogers look of bewilderment became even more so. "What does that mean?"

"It means that while the work we're doing is certainly not simple, the reason is. You heard Jebumo. He's offering a way to save our planet, and us. It's that simple. We knew it wouldn't be easy." John put his hand on Rogers' shoulder. "We've had challenges before, you and I. I don't even need to say that this is obviously the biggest and most important yet. Just think about what we're doing man."

Rogers took a breath and exhaled. "You're right, John. I just…" he stopped and shook his head. "Are you sure about what you're about to do? I mean, Christ, this is beyond Star Trek and Star Wars put together."

John laughed. "I am sure. I've never been more sure about anything in my life. It's as if I knew this was going to happen.." He gestured toward the chamber taking shape. "It is like something out of a sci-fi movie, but I believe it. I know it. Don't ask me how, but I do." He gazed at the chamber. "And I couldn't do it without you. We're almost there. Are you still with me?"

Rogers shook his head, almost appearing guilty of something. "Of course I am, John. Besides, it's your neck." He laughed.

"Okay. Want me to talk to the others?"

"No, they'll be fine. They just sometime think about what we're actually doing and it is so incredible, it's a little overwhelming. I'll feed'em some more nuts."

John roared with laughter. "Good idea." He started walking away, then turned and said over his shoulder, "How about a good movie tonight? I was thinking 2001: A Space Odessy."

Rogers waved his hand in dismissal as he shook his head.

John left the lab but could not shake the uneasy feeling he had regarding snatches of the argument he had heard.

Though Rogers had dismissed the discussion as routine, it had sounded far from that. Allatos Stanton, a brilliant and normally soft spoken scientist had seemed very firm about what he was saying.

John's concern and curiosity had not subsided by the time he reached his quarters, so he decided he needed to know more.

He entered the house and went directly to his 'spy room,' as Viktor called it. The room was full of video monitors showing all the labs and work areas. John did not consider it spying, but rather a way to keep up with the work going on in several different locations. He couldn't be everywhere at once, and this allowed him to pick and choose where he should be on any given day. The videos also recorded, so he could catch up on projects when he returned from his many trips.

He sat down behind the lab monitor that had recorded the discussion he had overheard and pulled up the time period of interest. It took only a few moments for John to learn that the argument between Rogers and Stanton had to do with the chamber transporter. Rogers obviously felt it was ready; Stanton did not.

"John, how about a little fishing." Viktor yelled out from inside the house.

"Viktor, glad you're here. Come to the video room."

"Spying again, huh?" Viktor joked as he entered.

"Listen to this." John replayed the last few minutes of the lab discussion between Rogers and Stanton.

Viktor listened carefully while John waited for his reaction. Viktor sat back with a contemplative look.

"What do you think?" John asked as he stopped the video.

Viktor continued staring at the now blank monitor.

John patiently watched his friend.

Viktor stood and walked to a window, gazing out. Finally he turned. "Well, it sounds to me like Allatos Stanton doesn't agree with your boy Rogers that the system is ready." He walked back to the monitor and looked at John. "It also sounds like Rogers is in a big hurry to move Stanton to another phase."

John knew that Viktor had never cared much for Rogers personally, so he let the 'boy' comment slide.

"What did Rogers say about the discussion?" Viktor added.

"I walked in on the tail end of the discussion, and he didn't really say anything. Actually made light of it. Passed it off as routine."

"I know you regard Stanton very highly, as do I. He has also been a key player in the projects' success so far." He leaned toward John. "You probably don't want to hear this, but I'd talk to Stanton if it were me. I know Rogers is your main guy, and you don't like to go around him, but it looks kinda funny to me."

John sat silent for a moment.

"You may be right." He finally responded. "A couple of things bother me. First of all, John Rogers has never kept anything from me. Just the opposite. He usually invites my feedback. This time he didn't even tell me the nature of the discussion. Very unusual."

"And number two?" Viktor asked when John did not continue.

"Allatos Stanton is a brilliant scientist and very much a team player. I can't imagine Rogers brushing him aside over what appeared to be Allatos's strong objections on the readiness issue. Rogers always err's on the side of caution, so this is totally out of character."

72

"I agree, and I'll add that Allatos is a real gentleman, very soft spoken. It was obvious how much he disagreed by his unusual tone. You should talk to him and find out what the big concern is. Besides, if you're worried about hurting Rogers' feelings, and I know you are, it isn't out of the ordinary for you to socialize with the other engineers and scientists. You do it all the time." Viktor said, seeing John's concern. "Besides, this has to do with the breaking apart of our bodies and getting the pieces back together again. I think it would be wise to make sure Rogers hasn't had a lapse in judgment." He added.

John laughed. "You're right. This is probably not the time to be overprotective of someone's feelings. I know Stanton usually goes to the north bluff after dinner. Told me one time it was quiet there, and he found it relaxing. Maybe I'll stroll out there this evening. Want to come along?"

"No, you're the one who speaks scientist. He might be more open if it's just the two of you."

"Okay. I'll let you know what happens."

"Sure you don't want to go fishing in the meantime?" Viktor asked.

"No. Think I'll review more of the laser and disk work to get a better feel for where we are."

"Thought so." Viktor said, not surprised. "Well, if I can't be of any help, I'm off to feed the fish."

"Go ahead. And thanks."

"Okay, John. See you later."

A few hours later, as predicted, John approached Allatos Stanton, who was gazing out over the vast ocean as it shimmered in the last light of day.

"Mister Klein, how good to see you." Stanton spoke without turning. "I've been expecting you."

"Great view here, Allatos." John moved next to the other man. "Why would you be expecting me?" 'And how did you know it was me,' John was thinking.

"You probably heard enough of our discussion this morning to be, if not concerned, then curious about the status of our project. We are, after all, at a critical juncture, and you are the one being teleported."

"You're right. I was curious, but I usually get John Rogers to fill me in when I have questions."

"I know, but here you are." Allatos quickly responded.

The two men stood quietly a few moments. Finally, John broke the silence.

"Well, I need to leave the island tomorrow for a day or two, so why don't you fill me in."

"Surely." Stanton said, as if expecting the request. "As you know, my team has been developing the disk-laser interface for the teleportation. Basically, as the R.P.M.'s of the disk increases, it is critical the laser system stay exactly in sync or the transport will fail."

"Yes, Jebumo was very specific about that." John interjected, recalling how Jebumo had stressed that point.

"Exactly. Well, Rogers says the system is ready and assigned my team to the next phase of the project. I told him the system is not ready, but I failed to convince him."

"But why would he do that? Are you sure it is not ready? I don't understand why Rogers would move forward if he had doubts."

"Absolutely sure. You and Viktor will not survive the teleportation if the system is used in its current state." Stanton replied emphatically.

"And what would it take to get it ready?"

"It's a matter of running the syncing programs and adjusting until it syncs. Probably one more day."

"One day!" John exclaimed. "Surely Rogers could give you one more day, even if he doesn't believe it is necessary." John shook his head. "I'm not sure I understand that."

Stanton did not respond.

John realized he was in a precarious position. Stanton was an expert in his field, but Rogers was the chief scientist and John's friend. They were so close to their goal, John simply did not want to cause disruptions at this point. Neither did he want to die in the chamber. Somehow, for reasons he couldn't really explain, he felt he could trust Stanton.

He made a decision.

"Tell you what. It could be that John Rogers needs a break. Think I'll take him with me tomorrow. I've done that before for certain meetings, as you know. We would be gone two days. Can you get the systems ready in that time?"

"Yes, I can. If I encounter a problem, I could confer with Jebumo."

"Jebumo!" John was surprised. "When have you talked to Jebumo?" As far as he knew, John was the only one who spoke with Jebumo.

"Well, I mean, with you gone, and given the importance of the situation, I thought if necessary, it would be warranted."

John studied the scientist. 'There's more here than I know', he thought.

"We can fix the problem and you will succeed." Stanton stated, as if reading John's mind.

"Okay." John said. "Guess I need to go see John Rogers. But Allatos, please understand that I'm doing this to put your mind at ease and on the off chance that John Rogers may have missed something. It doesn't change the fact that John is the lead scientist."

"Of course. Some intervention, no matter how slight, is sometimes required to manage a situation."

John was taken aback slightly. Hearing that sentiment sounded familiar.

He offered his hand to Stanton. "Okay, Allatos, I will leave you to your meditation."

John felt comfortable with Allatos Stanton, and maybe John Rogers did indeed just need a break.

Upon his return to the compound, John advised Rogers that he needed him on the trip, and after some objection, Rogers reluctantly agreed to his boss's request.

Two days later, back on the island, John called Viktor, whom he had asked to monitor things in his absence, to get a status check. Always, the humorist, Viktor's response was short.

"Ready to energize, Captain."

Finally, all was ready and the day had come for them to depart. John studied his friend.

"How are you doing Viktor? Are you nervous?"

"I feel exactly the same as you. We both love adventure and this should be the biggest adventure ever known to man. I'm very excited." He smiled. "You know, the moment we leave our planet, living on Earth will never be the same."

He paused and looked around, then continued. "I have always been a sailor, and adventure is in my blood, but I never imagined I would ever experience this level of

76

adventure in my lifetime. I say, let's go for it, and may the force be with us!"

John laughed, slapped his good friend on the shoulder and told him he was feeling the same exact anticipation.

They stepped into the chamber at 9 a.m. after saying goodbye to all the staff. Almost in unison, they took one last glimpse at the blue sky above them, took in every detail of the space around them. They were ready. The time had come.

They stepped onto the disks and gave a thumbs-up to John Rogers. The disks started to spin as the laser started flashing until a steady stream of light seemed to cover both of them. Then, in a flash, and with a small rumble, they were gone.

Even though the crew knew what was supposed to happen, it was hard to believe until it really did. Those left behind stood riveted in stunned silence. They all wondered if John and Viktor would ever return. John had left very complete instructions to be followed if he and Viktor didn't return and though they all knew that, they could not wrap their brains around what they had just witnessed. It wasn't science fiction, it had really happened. Two human beings had disappeared before their very eyes.

John had told them he'd "call" to tell them he was all right just as soon as he could.

All they could do now was wait.

CHAPTER TEN
THE OBSERVERS

Allatos Stanton gazed across the endless water. Dim moonlight poured down, reflecting over the calm surface. On such nights he particularly enjoyed this place on the high bluff. During the first few months of work on the island project, others had frequented his special place, so he would come later, when they had all gone to bed. Now, almost five years later, his fellow engineers and scientists had long since become bored with this quiet bluff; this place of solitude. It was the way of earthlings. Boredom. Not truly understanding quiet places as an opportunity to simply be. To look inside.

He found that to be particularly true of engineers and scientists involved in projects—in problem solving. A single-mindedness that would not comfortably allow the interference of passiveness. Some even had frequent sleep problems because, in their jargon, their minds wouldn't leave the problem at hand.

Earth was the third planet to which Allatos had been sent from Plytar. Jebumo and the council chose observers carefully, and those chosen could decline without question. Though few did, it was always their choice. Part of the evolved philosophy of Plytar was an innate knowledge that a choice on any matter could be made without discussion or explanation.

It intrigued him that earthlings could not seem to give an answer without an accompanying explanation or excuse. Even when none was sought or required.

He did like them. In his role as one of many hired scientists, Allatos knew he was not among typical earthlings. A person who would leave everything to work on an island for five years was probably more curious and adventuresome than most others. But still, they all had their peculiar ways.

"A famous Earth philosopher once wrote, 'if a tree falls in the forest and no one hears it, does it make a sound?"

Allatos was aware that Sirta was behind him but also knew she would speak when ready.

He turned with a smile. "I am pleased but not surprised to see you, Sirta."

She returned his smile. "Now that you have lived among earthlings, how do they answer that question?"

"As you know well, they answer in many ways, which must please the philosopher whose obvious intent was to evoke discussion as opposed to a logical, deductive answer."

"Yes, and I believe it speaks to the curious nature of these beings. I so enjoyed that about them during my time here."

Sirta glanced up into the velvety blackness of the sky.

Allatos turned to follow her gaze.

In the vast distance, a tiny blue-green spark was streaking across the sky. He knew the spark was trailing a medium size spacecraft because of the barely discernible, intermittent, soft, diffused illumination.

He mentally extrapolated the ships trajectory.

"Could be Cantaureans." Allatos stated matter-of-factly.

The Cantaureans were from a planet of poor resources, but inhabited by a strong-willed race. They made their living by fighting others planet's battles. All good generals know that the winner in most wars is the one who makes fewer mistakes than his enemy. The Cantaureans evolved a tactical culture based on a strategy that develops the best tactics for inducing mistakes. War, in many forms, was their livelihood, and their services went to the highest bidder.

"There will always be those who try to stop our transformations; on the planet being transformed and those who hire the warriors." Sirta said.

"Yes, I have seen them before while I have been on the island. They could know of our involvement, but so far, they have not come any nearer to the planet, and I have not seen any drones dropped. The Earth's governments always explain their presence as meteor's even though their course and altitude is always the same. They are very secretive about it."

He turned back to Sirta.

"I'm not sure why the government's on this planet don't share their limited knowledge of occasional interplanetary visits."

It is part of the primary reason the council decided to intervene here. A small number of powerful people making decisions that don't always seem to support the masses." She studied Allatos for a moment and continued.

"Jebumo advised me of your report regarding the near design failure of the chamber, but he did not send me here."

"You spent many years on Earth with your grandson, living among earthlings." Allatos replied in an understanding manner. "I suspect John and his group have surpassed even Jebumo's expectations," he added.

"Sirta glanced toward the sky again, turned and looked back toward the project complex.

"Of course we cannot directly interfere to alter the outcome of the transformation, which in this instance was not necessary."

"That is correct. John sought me out and made all decisions. I did no more or no less than that expected of me as a project engineer. The grandson of Sirta is very astute."

Sirta turned away from the complex. "Still, the council's decision to seed this planet and now to make contact with John was necessitated by the fact that there are powerful, corrupt earthling's who will take whatever measures necessary to protect their status."

"Perhaps they are already at work." Allatos replied. "John Klein is a driven man, very capable." He paused, studying Sirta. "You did well," he added.

"Not I. John's father and grandfather were not just intelligent. They were compassionate, fair men. Wonderful role models for a young John. He learned much and his actions so far attest to that."

"Still, this is not simply another planet to be transformed. To you, it is more. Understandably. You are concerned."

"All transformations are important. But yes, I confess I feel more involvement, and I am worried. It's a strange sensation." Sirta said.

"What would you have me do?" he asked.

Sirta smiled. "I have feelings that are hard for me to understand. Maybe I was too long with the earthling's."

They both laughed.

"Had it not been for you, the transporter would almost certainly fail. Maybe what you discovered was an oversight, or maybe the corruptors are at work. I know you cannot directly interfere. It is not our way, but..." Sirta's voice trailed off as she struggled with her feelings.

"Sirta, I will not interfere, but I will continue to watch and check carefully." He paused. "John will succeed. We are within hours of teleportation." He reached out and touched Sirta's arm. "Will you see him after he and Viktor arrive on Plytar?" he asked.

"Oh yes. Jebumo has already suggested that I do."

"He's down there. In the complex." Allatos said.

"I know." She looked thoughtful as she considered Allatos' veiled suggestion. "But he has much on his mind, and I must return."

"Yes, I understand. You said Jebumo did not send you, but does he wish something of me?"

"Yes, he would have you stay after the transformation to assist the scientist's for a period of time."

"I will." He reached out and took Sirta's hands. "I miss Plytar. I am happy you came."

Sirta smiled, released his hands, floated up and disappeared into the night sky.

CHAPTER ELEVEN

THE ENCOUNTER

John and Viktor were transported to a chamber on the far north side of Jebumo's planet, similar to Earth's North Pole. They were suspended in the atmosphere in the first of two chambers. In the entry chamber, they were checked out, then lifted to the next chamber. That chamber was designed to change them from their earthly form into Plytar form.

The entire planet had an invisible protection shield and the only way a life form could enter was through the chambers. This was necessary because there was still too much bad DNA throughout the universe and they had to protect themselves.

The second chamber was the critical key in the process. If you made it to the first chamber and you did not agree to go through the transformation, you were not allowed on the planet. There were *no* exceptions. You were also told that after your visit you would be put back into your original state. In this way, they protected their planet from invasion and contamination.

The planet's defense shield could not be penetrated by anything because any outside form would be reflected back into the universe.

Should expected 'guests' arrive in spacecraft, rather than being transported from their planets, the craft was required to remain in orbit while occupants were transported to the chamber. A craft attempting to enter the planet's atmosphere simply found itself back at its point of origin.

The inhabitants of Plytar were not interested in destroying anything or harming anyone, so making a protective shield that reflected whatever was sent back to its source made the most sense. They had used that procedure for millenniums.

The two men entered the second chamber and removed their clothing as instructed. In moments, a small amount of some form of gas was released, and the transformation began. The process took about three minutes to complete, after which their bodies took on new forms and both of them had the metabolism of a thirty-year-old.

Their bodies were like Jell-O but at the same time had an elastic quality. They could push their finger into their hand and it would seem to go through, then stop. When the finger was withdrawn, the hand would pop back into shape. This was true of the entire body. There was no effort required to move limbs.

When walking, they literally felt like they were walking on air because they could not feel anything beneath their feet. They just glided along effortlessly. They felt no aches or pains and had the most amazing vision and hearing. They could see things miles away with perfect clarity and their ears were fine-tuned receptors. Every sound was heard as if through the best set of headphones ever made.

Music was magical, and when spoken to, the voice of the other person had a musical quality to it. Hearing others sing created the sensation that every molecule of your body had come alive and you were the song and the song was you. Music bathed the entire body in pure joy and caused it to vibrate like a tuning fork.

John and Viktor had been told before they left earth they would see and feel things on Plytar which in their earth form, they could not fully comprehend. While Jebumo had described some of the sensory changes they would experience, only now that they were here did the change fully register.

Through a process they could not yet understand, they suddenly knew what life in this world was like. What they now saw, felt, heard, experienced seemed almost normal, though they retained their earth memory. It seemed they knew all the amazing, unbelievable conditions and possibilities of this unique world. Yet, they remembered daily life on earth, which made what they instantly knew about this place even more amazing.

   ***

On Plytar, all senses were so heightened that one felt a part of everything. The concept of cultural norms, so ingrained in every ethnic group on earth, did not exist here. Because of this, inhibitions did not exist. Sex, for example, was enjoyed by all beings because there were no inhibitions or rules. If you felt like having sex and someone was also so inclined, you consummated and moved on. It was not uncommon for groups of beings to get together and have sex for hours. One also had the ability to change sex at will and transform into any form desired. If you wanted to be a bird for a period of time, all you had to do was imagine yourself as a bird and wish for it.

This phenomenon applied to all living things, both on the land and in the sea. Every being believed that *everything is*, and knew they were part of everything. All living things communicated with each other. If you went walking with a dog, or saw a bird, or swam with the fish, you communicated without talking and everything was fully understood. Words were seldom used because of the belief that words fell short of true feelings. Feelings were best communicated with the eyes and through touch.

There were opinions and difference of opinions but not 'hurt feelings', because all opinions mattered and were shared.

Sickness did not exist. The body was similar to the gills on the fish. A membrane took in all the nutrients it needed from the atmosphere through both the mouth and the skin. It was a process that occurred naturally, requiring no thought or planning. No living creature or plant was consumed and plants regenerated perpetually. This was similar to some plants on earth that are never watered or fed. Jebumo's world had evolved to the point that one didn't even have to drink water because the humidity was seventy-five percent and the body absorbed all it needed.

Blooming plants gave off nutrients that entered the atmosphere in a pure state. This in turn was absorbed in such a way that there was no waste. Everything was consumed. If one desired a special taste, they simply sat in Plytar's version of a restaurant located in selected fields and captured that particular essence as it was admitted into the air. Food was never cooked and that lowered energy consumption.

All energy came from the wind, sun, waterfalls, and ocean wave movement so there was never any pollution. No need for bathrooms or sewer treatment plants because there wasn't any waste. Talking was kept to a minimum because your thoughts could be read by any other person. This in turn also kept the air more purified. Transportation using any form of mechanical vehicle did not exist. All one had to do was think of the destination desired and they were there.

To leave the planet you had to go through the chambers, but this rarely happened because there wasn't any other place you would rather be than where you are. Life just kept happening spontaneously. If you wanted to build something, you built it. If you wanted to invent something, you invented it. Money in any form did not exist. Therefore, neither did greed and power struggles. Everyone lived forever in perpetual peace and harmony. Plytar inhabitants enjoyed a state of mind that earth poets and philosophers wrote about for centuries, but could not achieve because of earth's rules, norms and taboos.

Science was important and many chose to be scientists. New forms of art were constantly being discovered and very large galleries could be found all over the planet. Museums, in a traditional sense, did not exist because of the belief that art was a living thing. When a certain form had reached its full potential, a new one was discovered or created. All believed that art was in everything they did and everyone was an artist no matter what they did.

Children were born and grew to the age of thirty, then stopped aging. If more space was required in the future there were plans in place to inhabit dead planets that were once inhabited by bad DNA.

Jebumo's world had the ability to change the bad atmosphere, build a shield, and make the planet a colony.

Birth control was not a problem. Many chose not to have children so it would not be a problem for many years to come. While parents provided the primary nurturing of children, all inhabitants participated in their growing and learning processes, not unlike many of earth's cultures did long ago; a sense of community upbringing, now replaced with 'not wanting to get involved'.

Never aging beyond thirty years was particularly incredible to John—not to even mention ever dying. At his age, he sometimes thought about the years he had left, as do most people at some point in their 'old age'. Though John had had a most successful life, measured by any number of yardsticks, he was no different than any other person in their so called twilight years. He still wanted to do things, have new experiences, meet new people, and create new things. Because of their age difference, Viktor thought less about his mortality, but he did think about it every now and again. No one on Plytar had such thoughts. Why would they when the concept of aging and dying was totally foreign . Eternity was theirs to do with as they chose. Likewise, boredom was not a possible state of mind because your mind was never without the possibility for new endeavors.

As that fact entered John's conscious thought, he felt an amazing sense of peace. Being able to do so much, anything, without fear of running out of time. A perpetual bucket list without limitations. It was euphoric to think about. Taxes, tangible things, law, policies—all earth things. Not applicable here.

Homes, hotels, or hospitals did not exist because there was no need for rest and no illness. There were numerous places where people gathered to discuss science, art, and to create. There was no government because everyone provided for everyone else. It was the natural order of things. No money or barter or possessions.

Everything that existed was for everyone to use. Rules and regulations were not needed because each being totally loved and respected the other. The concept of animosity did not exist. There was no one thing to have faith in because all believed in everything and lived through an unwritten code of mutual respect.

Jebumo's life was dedicated to purifying all the universes of bad DNA. He had been doing it for countless years, and he would not stop until all the contaminated DNA did not exist. He knew if he just waited, these planets would eventually disintegrate, but he was concerned that some would evolve to the point that they could escape and infect other planets. Earth was a good example. He was determined to continue until his job was finished.

His primary focus was on those who reached out for help, and at any given time he could have a dozen or more planets to work with. He knew also that if this work was going to end any time in the foreseeable future, he had to recruit other clean planets to do the same work he was doing. He felt John Klein was a being who would join him in this kind of mission, and he was eager to get him on board. Sirta's DNA transference had proved its value many times over the millenniums and he was confident this time would be no different. He knew that once Earth was transformed, a man like John, with the help of Viktor, would take on the challenge of transforming other planets until there was no more bad DNA.

The vastness of space makes it impossible to even imagine that Jebumo, or any entity, could believe they could rid the universe of all bad DNA, but he felt it was worth it because as with any sickness, it weakened all around it. Jebumo was a great scientist who should've been working on other projects, and in time, he would, because he also knew he would live forever. He did have a strong desire to create and was hopeful that someone like John Klein would eventually take over for him for a period of time so he could work on other science projects.

John and Viktor completed the transforming stage and began a slow descent to the ground followed by poking each other's body. They were amazed by the change in their voices and vision and how easy it was for them to walk or as it were, glide. It was exhilarating being thirty again, but this time without any sensation of anxiety, hunger, or pain in any form. Because they hadn't seen their wives for months, they emitted a powerful aura of sensuality. As women and men gathered around them and brushed against John and Viktor's bodies, the men experienced instant orgasms.

Jebumo stood back and watched until the initial contact subsided, then he approached and introduced himself.

They all took a moment to look into each other's eyes. Immediately, a sense of peace and love came over them. No words were spoken for several moments as the impact of what was happening settled in.

"I have a surprise for you," Jebumo said to John. "Someone is waiting to meet you."

John was curious because he couldn't imagine what his host was talking about. His confusion lessened when a beautiful, slender woman approached. She looked familiar, but John wasn't sure just why or who she was until she looked into his eyes.

It was his grandmother Sirta, whom he had always loved dearly.

As a small child, she constantly filled his head with science and they did many projects together. He was much closer to her than his own mother. They fell into a long embrace.

"Welcome, John," she said as she pulled away and gazed into his eyes.

John was overcome with joy. "How are you here? I don't understand."

She smiled. "I have always been here, but also on Earth with you for a period of time."

"But I always felt you were with me, even though you weren't."

"Oh, but I was," she replied. "I have never left you. You just couldn't see me."

John now understood. "All those dreams, all the times the right thought would pop into my head—that was you."

Sirta laughed. "Well, partly. You are an important part of the future of your world, so I was something akin to what you might call a 'guardian angel'. But, it was you who made your own way through life and achieved success. We are all alike, but in unique ways, very different, and though you were fathered by humans, the DNA of our people flows through you. Now, you have joined us, as soon all of Earth will."

"What about my father?" he asked.

"He's with us, though right now he's in another galaxy helping Jebumo get rid of bad DNA. You'll see him soon enough."

***

John now realized that his blood and DNA must be from this planet; from these beings. It all started to make sense.

He knew he had inherited Tesla's blood from an amazingly smart grandmother. This could explain why he had always been so inventive. Yet, he always wondered why so many of his thoughts and inventions came to him in dreams. Now he knew. It was Sirta. He would see entire inventions completed and working. His ability to see the future was one of his biggest assets and the main reason he was able to amass so much wealth.

All of this was a grand plan put in motion by Jebumo when he came upon Earth and realized it needed help because it was falling apart.

John jerked out of his thoughts when Jebumo laid his hand on his shoulder with a knowing look.

"There is much yet to talk about, but I must first show you something."

Both men nodded in anticipation.

"As I told you before you left Earth, we are involved with correcting bad DNA of planet inhabitants throughout many universes'. You are an example of how we do this."

"What do you mean, exactly?" John asked.

"It is necessary for an inhabitant of an affected planet to cause the change. Through a seeding process, we integrate our DNA with that of a selected being, and if their original DNA is not too corrupted, they effect the change by spreading our essence."

"But surely you help in some way." John interrupted.

"Our way is to only provide the means, and never interfere to any significant degree."

"So you do help on some scale."

Jebumo smiled. "The answer to that is not simple, and you may find it hard to understand or accept. While we do not interfere once seeding is done, we do, on rare occasions 'manage' situations. It is important that you understand the difference."

John and Viktor exchanged looks. Both were confused. "I'm not sure we do," John said.

Jebumo continued. "You are here now because we caused a time shift in your universe to allow you to reconsider abandoning your, and our, project." He paused a moment. "We intervened, but ultimately, you made the decision to continue. Had you not done so, we would have abandoned this mission." He gave a knowing look. "I should add that we were very confident you would do the right thing."

"But if a planet is worth seeding, why wouldn't you go all out to ensure that it works?" John asked.

"There must be enough good original DNA in the chosen being to cause the desire to change to happen. Our DNA only provides the capacity. There are some planets whose inhabitants are beyond hope; their DNA is too corrupted, and even if we were to locate a possibility, their odds of succeeding would be very small because it is so widespread."

"What do you do in those cases?" Viktor asked.

"The short answer is nothing. We could easily destroy those planets, but that is not our way. In those cases, we do what we can through 'managed' intervention to protect our and other planets from them, and eventually they destroy themselves."

"So you do intervene, but inconspicuously. That's what you mean when you say manage." John said, more as a statement than question.

"We do when it is helpful to one of our own close to the situation or an innocent planet's survival is at risk, or the threat of spreading bad DNA is imminent. I can best show you by example."

Jebumo waved his arm and three dimensional images appeared before them. Three figures in spacesuits emerged from a spacecraft of some sort and were traversing across a rocky, rugged looking landscape.

"This is an event that happened long ago, but you will be seeing it as if it were happening in real time. Two of these beings were from a very corrupt planet; beyond saving. Their inhabitants raided other planets, killed or enslaved the beings there and conducted mining operations until the planet was ruined. The remaining inhabitants of the ruined planet, those fortunate enough to have survived, soon died off because the planet's resources had been exhausted or destroyed." Jebumo paused and let this information sink in.

"The third figure is a scientist, Gutar, from our planet. When we became aware the raiders were planning a mission to this small, defenseless planet, we intervened by inserting Gutar who, through powers we possess, became the mission's mineral analysis expert. Watch and listen."

The three men in spacesuits were making their way across very inhospitable terrain toward a large, volcano appearing mountain. Two held some sort of weapon and the third, obviously Gutar, carried various instruments contained in protective satchels.

They arrived at the base of the mountain and entered an opening which had been mapped by their equipment upon landing.

The tunnel went a very long way and joined several other offshoots. It was not pitch black dark as one might expect in a tunnel, and they could see reasonably well without lights. How this was possible, they were not sure.

"Are you getting anything yet?" the team leader asked.

"No, nothing of value," replied Gutar, who had been scanning for worthwhile minerals. "I told you it was doubtful there would be anything worth our time here." He added.

"Yeah, well, we're here. Let's go further in."

"I'm telling you I think we're wasting our time," Gutar responded.

The team leader, agitated, stopped and faced Gutar. "You just do your job. We just got started. Besides, I need a new find bonus. Come on." The team started off again.

They had gone barely another three hundred feet into the semidarkness when the team leader whispered, "stop!" in a tone that sends chills through one's body. The men froze in place.

At first, there was only silence except what sounded like the distant dripping of water. Then, suddenly, there was a padding sound behind the group. The sound stopped as they turned, then started again, perhaps thirty feet away.

"There's something behind us. Must have followed us in." The team leader said as he snapped on his external helmet light.

Several feet away, blinking in the sudden light stood a large eyed two legged creature. Though in a bent position, he appeared to be no more than four feet tall. He didn't seem to have any hair or wrinkles on his body and had a pale hue one might expect from underground living. He did not appear to be frightened in the least. This was obvious by the huge grin on his unusual looking face. He approached the three men with long claw-hands outstretched, as if in a greeting. The team leader warned him to stop, but the creature responded by grinning even bigger and uttering a faint whimpering sound.

The team leader shot him dead with no further warning.

The creature clutched his belly and yelped in pain. Just as he was about to die, he looked up at the men and smiled. His face relaxed into a peaceful expression, as if he were full of joy.

"Why did you do that? He obviously did not mean us any harm." Gutar said, as he bent to check the creature for signs of life.

"Who asked your opinion? Besides, I didn't like the looks of those claws." He gave Gutar a dirty look. "Quit wasting time with him. Come on. Let's go further in."

After they had walked a few more minutes, more light could be seen ahead, and the tunnel seemed to open up more. In the distance, a sound like something calling could be heard, with what were probably responses replying back.

The group arrived at the larger opening and peered down a slight incline into a large cavern resembling a huge deep room where several tunnel offshoots met. A strange scene was playing out before them. Several of the creatures were dancing about, hugging each other, as if celebrating some wonderful event. They would jump up, fall to the ground, and disappear under some type of vegetation, and then jump up again, all the while making childlike, guttural noises and grinning. As the commotion continued, a steady stream of creatures entered the opening from adjoining tunnels and joined the activity.

Many of the creatures held their hands up toward the three men in what may have been a welcoming gesture.

"What the hell are they doing?" The team leader exclaimed.

"It looks like they're dancing, and perhaps extending their hands out to us is their way of inviting us to join them." Gutar responded. He glanced at some of his meters. "I'm getting nothing on my analysis meters. Just your basic dead rock. Let's get out of here. We've wasted enough time." He added, before the team leader decided to get trigger happy again.

Before the team leader could respond, a smaller creature, obviously a child, came toward the group, beating little claws together while uttering the whimpering like noise. The team leader shoved the toddler over with the point of his weapon and laughed. The child, thinking it was a game, grabbed the end of the barrel and grinned up at the man.

What was probably the child's mother approached and scooped up the youngster. She made a chirping noise at her charge, then extended one arm toward the men and grinned.

Without hesitation, the other team member fired a burst into her chest. She fell with a soft thud and lay still.

John and Viktor watched in dismay as the scene before them continued to play out.

The baby, clearly not understanding, stood and held his arms out to the men, smiling all the while.

"Dumb little asshole, ain't he?" The team leader said as he raised his weapon in preparation to fire.

Gutar quickly turned, bumping the would be murderer, and headed back the way they had come, as he said, "I'm leaving. As the team scientist, I'm declaring there is nothing on this rock worthwhile. We were not sent here for target practice and we're wasting time."

The team leader glared at Gutar's retreating back and then turned back to the child, who had started scampering down the incline to join the party. He uttered a string of profanities and hurried after the other two men.

John and Viktor stood dumbfounded as the landing team disappeared and the images faded away.

"I can't believe anyone could be so cruel. What happened to those creatures?" Viktor asked.

"This is a primitive, humanoid race that live a life of simple bliss. They have not evolved, as your race and others did, for thousands of Earth's years. They want nothing more than what they have and continue to live in their simple, happy state. Because they are happy, they seek nothing beyond that. It is bliss in its purest, most simple form."

"And what about the other guys?" John said.

"The race seeking to pillage the land of these docile creatures were fortunately dissuaded by Gutar's false report that there was nothing on the planet worthwhile to their mining ventures."

Jebumo shook his head sadly and continued, "The pillager's have long since destroyed themselves. We could not help them, but this minor intervention saved those they would have destroyed."

"It may be terrible to even say, but based on their actions in what we just saw, I'd say the universe is probably better off without a race like that." Viktor stated.

Jebumo studied the two men. "There are many on your own planet who are doing the same thing. They raid and steal the resources of other countries causing internal wars and deprivation , and when their greed is satisfied, they move to the next country. Your people are not yet as ruthless as those you have just seen, but they are very close."

"My God, he's right." John exclaimed and looked at Viktor, who shook his head sadly in agreement.

"WE", Jubumo gestured toward the two men and continued," are about to change the direction your planet is heading. We could have infused our DNA into these wonderful creatures we just saw, and they would have advanced, discovered new things; changed. But to what end? They live in total bliss, so there is nothing more they need. Unlike your people."

John looked thoughtful. "Once given the way, we control our own destiny. It's not up to any other person or race to do it for us."

"Exactly. Our DNA opens the door, and we sometimes adjust situations if necessary, but in the end, you succeed or fail on your own. It is critical in the beginning that our choice for seeding be the right one. You have proven yourself on this project because you believe. You now most understand that as you continue, we cannot be of much help."

Jebumo paused and looked from one man to the other. "You are very close to attaining the goal—yours and ours. What you see and learn here on Plytar will reinforce your will to succeed and give you the knowledge to do so. When you leave, the destiny of your planet is in your hands."

CHAPTER TWELVE

TOUR

Jebumo suggested they take a tour of the surrounding areas before they began discussions about their mission. After inquiring about after effects from their long journey, followed by both men's assurance that they were fine, they all set off on "foot."

It was amazing not to see any shopping centers, tall buildings, or factories, at least in the sense that we know those structures. No cars or trains, buses or planes. No vehicles of any kind.The landscape was mostly gentle, rolling hills, broken by slightly larger formations occasionally and dotted by small to medium trees and plants here and there.

A bird landed on John's shoulder and asked him if he liked the planet so far and then flew away after a swan dive around the group.

Plytar did not have libraries in the literal sense. Instead, giant computer centers were strategically located throughout the planet. In these centers one had only to put their hands on a console and ask a question. Once the answer was given, you never forgot it because it went into your own memory bank. Likewise, if another being had a question and you had the answer, all he had to do was hold your hand and the answer was transferred.

The planet's air was pure, with a very slight hint of mint. Everything was amazingly clean, because there wasn't any garbage or waste. Flying over terrain free of waste landfills, auto junkyards, factory complexes and other trappings found on earth was very refreshing to the two men.

As they traveled, they passed beings gathered together in what looked like friendly conversation, yet no one was talking. Dogs, cats and a variety of other animals contributed as well. Jebumo explained that living things were sharing in life as equals.

"While animals and humans may not share that many interests, they do enjoy hearing about the other's interests and activities."

Is this heaven? John thought to himself. An answer came back almost as soon as he thought it.

"Yes, and it has been here for all time. Earth human's concept of heaven, regardless of religion—and as you know, there are many, is that if you act a certain way, you will enter it when you die. Here, we live in what many earthlings might call heaven. It is not a reward; it is our way of life."

John commented that all the trees and flowers seemed to be in full bloom. Jebumo replied that he was correct, that flowering plants were meant to have flowers all the time, not just part time.

John and Viktor saw beings coming together in what appeared to be waves and then quickly separating. In just a moment, one would appear and then in another, disappear. They both wondered where everyone was going and coming from. Jebumo replied that they should join them and find out. To their amazement, they discovered that the activity was similar to strolling a large building with several different discussions being conducted in its many rooms. When you heard something of interest in passing, you may go in and listen. This was the activity in progress here except, no buildings. When a passing person had thoughts of interest, you took off with him to learn more.

The sky on Plytar was green instead of blue, and everyone could see a sun although Plytar did not have a sun. Jebumo explained that the light shone all the time, and there were no clouds. Their sun had burned out years ago and they devised a way to survive without it by inventing and erecting a shield that captured light from distant stars and magnified it. The intensity of the rays was mild compared to a sun and remained constant so there was never any harmful effects on the living things.

There were no streets, paths, or sidewalks because they were not necessary. When the people on Plytar moved, their feet did not touch the ground. You felt the sensation of the ground under you, but you never touched. If you felt like moving faster, you just picked up your pace and quickly attained the speed you deemed necessary. There was a protective screen around you that kept you from hitting any other object. Beings flew around in all directions and never collided. The sky was full of them and they were in all forms.

"What if I were here and I had an overwhelming urge to be in a car, speeding around the countryside?" John caught himself. "Opps. Guess I didn't need to speak."

Jubumo laughed out loud. "No, not at all. If you choose to speak, please do so. We do on occasion even though because our thoughts transfer, we don't need to. You could have the sports car that I know you are so fond of. It would be different and certainly not made of metal or have an internal combustion engine. You could create the car of your dreams and go as fast as you please without harming the environment by leaving rusting remains years hence. We'll be visiting a creative area later, and this will become more clear."

The region they were in was very lush and abundant. They were told larger animals were further south and lived in perfect harmony. Occasionally, you would see a transparent building that housed great laboratories containing works of art. There were no formal schools because everyone was self-taught. This would seem very strange on earth where school is so structured. Earth researchers know that children naturally learn most fully and deeply, and with greatest enthusiasm, in conditions that are almost opposite to those of the schools. The teach and test method employed there, in which learning is motivated by a system of rewards and punishments rather than by curiosity or by any real desire to know, is well designed for indoctrination and obedience training but not much else. John's thoughts were picked up by Jebumo.

"Your Albert Einstein said he hated school and learned despite of it and not because of it. Your Earth children, before school age, through their own efforts, figure out how to walk, run, jump, and climb. They learn their native language, and learn to assert their will, argue, amuse, question. They acquire an enormous amount of knowledge about the physical and social world around them. They do all this before anyone, in any systematic way, tries to teach them anything. That amazing capacity and desire to learn is then turned off with your coercive system of schooling. It's very different here."

Jebumo was referring to the fact that his planet inhabitants were born with great intelligence equal to many PhD's on Earth. Further study was accomplished in areas of interest by going to the computer centers. These supercomputers were constantly updated in nanoseconds. At any time, one could switch their attention from science to art and back to science by just wishing it. Everyone contributed as their own inclination dictated but so much was already known and provided for that no one needed to contribute anything else.

No one depended on anyone or anything because everything on the planet was self-generated and everyone participated as a normal process, not because of pressure to do so. In this way, all needs were met in reciprocal fashion. Peace and order had been in place for billions and billions of years and now was just a way of life.

There was no history of the planet because it had always been this way. There had been no evolution. Plytar was born out of pure thought of how things should be and never mutated or became infected by the bad DNA. John wondered how this could possibly happen. Maybe there was a supreme being, or thing, or something that caused it. On the other hand, how was he and Viktor even here, on this incredible journey? Maybe what IS should not be questioned, could not be questioned, because there is no answer—there is just IS. It was obvious it worked here.

No one ever desired to be in control or thought they should pray to a more supreme being than their way of life. Because of this, they were never ruined or ruled by organized religion with all its rules and hypocrisy. The masses had no need to be controlled by religion or governments so there weren't any. They realized that they all were units of energy and that by being here they had always been here. They could take any number of forms, and they would still always be here. Inhabitants knew that in time all other planets would evolve and be like them. They accepted there is no end of time for anything, so eventually everything evolves for good because there is more positive energy than negative in all the universes.

John asked Jebumo if they could see other parts of the planet. Jebumo agreed and told John and Viktor how they would travel. He explained the process where all one had to do was bend about thirty degrees at the waist, or to the point where if you went any further, you would fall down. Then think about where you wanted to go and say it. In a flash, when everything was clear around you, you would be off. He cautioned them that the people of Plytar grew into this ability as children, not unlike earthlings learning to walk. Therefore, they should proceed slowly and experiment.

Viktor gave it a try, leaned too far and pitched forward, but instead of falling, he did a complete circle and started again. John joined him and after a few rough starts and much laughter, to the delight of those who gathered to watch, they figured it out.

They were going to a province halfway around the planet. Its name was Yogat, and it was the hub of their Arts Center. As they began their journey, they passed miles of orchards and fields of flowers. Everything was in perpetual bloom, and you could see and feel the essence they gave off in the air. It was this way all over the planet, and you could actually feed yourself as you traveled.

Here, the mouth was used primarily for breathing, not eating; the skin absorbed all the nutrients it needed as it passed over the land. Most of the time, you did not have to think about eating, but if you were hungry, you just flew a few meters out of town and did a quick pass over a field and your hunger was quickly satisfied. The body had its own system of not letting in any more nutrients once your hunger diminished. Therefore, no one was overweight and everyone was extremely healthy.

The use of GMO's or fertilizers were unheard of, so everything was organic. Natural was the way it had always been from the start of the planet's inception, whenever that was. The inhabitants were not sure just how they came to the planet or how they had evolved. Everything just always seemed to exist for all time. In fact, time was not a concept they measured or even thought about. They were immortal, the light shone constantly, so there was no day and night as we know it.

Why think about time or preserve it when there was only the moment, the *now*. The past or future had no meaning. You were born into the world and in moments you were the equivalent of Earth's thirty, the age you maintained for all time. There was no need or desire to bother with something that had no meaning and literally was a waste of time.

They arrived at Yogart in moments, or so it seemed. The smells and sights they had passed were still fresh in their heads and they were completely nourished.

The City was full of the most amazing architecture one could ever imagine. Every building was a piece of art, painted in a maze of colors with twists and turns that went off in multiple directions. Some defied gravity, but on close inspection one could see a very fine clear line holding the structures together. PlayArt had been a form here for many centuries. Buildings, for lack of a better description, contained interactive installations that went beyond anything ever seen on Earth.

They had evolved to appreciate art as something to be consumed, not just looked at. It was one thing simply to look at art, but quite another to actually be interactive with it.

Entry to these installations was through a chamber usually eight feet by eight feet, though some were much larger, and others might be an entire building. The smaller installations were most popular. As one stepped inside and entered a chamber, the art sensed your presence and knew whether or not you had ever been there before. As it analyzed who you were, your body temperature and aura were read.

Once the system was 'loaded' with your aura, you took up a position on a rotating disk and, like an orchestra conductor, when you pointed your hands, the environment responded to you. Through the use of video cameras, your movements were choreographed to music and the motion of the art. So when you pointed up or down, the artwork would move in unison and at the same time music would respond directly to your movements. Even though the art was there, already created, it became unique to the person 'leading the orchestra.' The entire experience was filmed and broadcast to anyone who might be interested. Likewise, you could coordinate ahead with a friend, and they could watch the entire process in real time.

The art used in these installations was what they called Painting With Light photographs. These were one second exposures where the photographer held the camera for a tenth of a second, moved the camera, and held it again for a tenth of a second. The lenses might be rotated at the same time or pumped if it was telephotic. The images were then projected onto a circular screen in front of the viewer. This then gave the participant endless images from which they could create their own art form.

The participant controlled the speed and special shoes kept them firmly connected to the disk no matter how fast they moved. From time to time, beings would spin up to twenty-five thousand revolutions per minute and become totally lost in what they were creating. The outside viewers saw only a blur, but to the participant it all happened in slow motion while they felt totally under control.

Sights and sounds blended together and became one with the body so it felt as if you were the music and you were the art, not the other way around. This in turn created states of extreme euphoria that could only be experienced in the chambers. John and Viktor quickly figured out why these chambers were the most popular PlayArt installations.

To be in a place that was all about playing, discovery, and creation had Viktor and Johns' head spinning. They both had the same thought; *if only our planet could have places to go like this, how different it would be. To play and create instead of fighting.*

The positive energy that would spread from such a place made John think of his friend Ernst Lurker who had asked him to fund a museum very similar to this, dedicated to PlayArt, which Ernst had invented in the seventies. He now felt sorry he did not do so but was optimistic that would change.

The group approached a building that seemed to be at least three-hundred stories high. The glass block structure twisted and turned as it rose from the ground. There was an opening at the top that was about ten feet in diameter. As they stood on a rotating disk, the entire building made a sound similar to that made when rubbing the top of a Champagne glass. The sound seemed to move up and down and back again as laser beams shot off in all directions and all angles throughout the building.

The disk began spinning and at the same time lowered itself seven stories into the ground. Jebumo said, "Skyward."

The spring-loaded disk, still spinning, was released, propelling the group at speeds over one-thousand miles per hour, straight through the building and into the atmosphere. Just as it seemed they would hit the protective shield, they stopped and slowly descended back down to the planet's surface. This process had been invented by a combined team of artists and scientists. It was called Stoned Immaculate because the experience caused a euphoric feeling of being reborn. It was as if your being was before you and behind you, and you were riding in the space between. There were no thoughts or attachments, just immaculate space where the traveler saw everything that is for what it is. As a result of speed and reflective light, there was a maze of colorful light designs that would cause the Earth's northern light show to pale in comparison. Upon descending, their senses were almost overwhelmed with what they had experienced.

Plytar was full of many different forms of PlayArt, both in buildings and built into the landscape, and while it seemed as though the city went on for many miles in all directions and offered much to delight the senses, Jebumo suggested there was much to see, so they should move on.

The next stop was the City of Mit, where the latest science was being discovered. They started moving and in an instant, had arrived. As with the last trip, they flew over fields of flowers and orchards until they reached the city limits. The designs of all the buildings in Mit were very different from Yogart and were so amazing nothing seemed real, no matter where you looked.

The structures seemed to be made out of glass, but on closer inspection it could be seen they were more like a membrane similar to that which made up the beings. The buildings were living things. They were all one-story high with vast expanses that seemed to stretch for miles with no supports. Along the perimeters, there were laboratories with the space in the middle left open for work and experiments.

Computer banks could be seen everywhere but without the typical hardware one would expect. Instead, thin flat membranes that resembled living organisms were interacting with the scientists, literally. There were no keyboards. The scientists talked to the membrane and it responded with perfect diction. They were even polite to each other and it seemed as though the computer was actually a coworker rather than a machine. Computers and scientists were aware they were teaching each other and getting smarter at the same time. All the computers on the planet were interconnected so they were constantly updated with the new knowledge being discovered. This link allowed the scientists to receive information relative to their project without the exhaustive stops to conduct research.

There was a building solely dedicated to inventing new PlayArt. The beings could never get enough, and the artists and scientists had the most fun working on these projects. Jebumo reminded them that here you could be anything for as long as you wanted to be. Some remained a scientist for millions of years, then perhaps a fish. There was always plenty of everything to do for everyone because nothing really ever *had* to be done. If one just wanted to be, then that is what one did. Some chose to just *be* and contemplate, so that is what they did.

Because on Earth there is a cultural mindset to constantly achieve, the concept of just *being* was very foreign to John and Viktor. But on Plytar, it was what *is*. Planet Earth beings had never grasped the reality that we all are and always have been, so why do we have to be anything? John had these thoughts and knew Viktor did as well, because they were allowed to think as humans and be in each other's head to get the full effect of their visit.

Jebumo announced they should now move on to the next stop on the tour, the City of Improvo, the main center for the discovery of new art. Their journey was a replica of the last, and soon they landed in the heart of the city where all the buildings were white with green, blue, pink, and orange accents. Stripes went up and down the walls, and odd shaped objects were placed in different spaces on the buildings and throughout landscapes.

Upon seeing this, John and Viktor smiled and then burst into laughter. There wasn't anything particularly funny about the place, it was just that it caused one to feel pure joy that became spontaneous laughter. The beings here all had very broad smiles on their faces all the time. Some looked ecstatic because they had just created a totally unique piece of art and nothing could compete with that level of joy.

Even though the beings here looked pretty much the same, each had an aura that was unique. It seemed to reflect each artist by a slightly different look and the way they carried themselves. The buildings ranged in size and shape from one story to seventy stories. Some covered several city blocks and had very tall ceilings resembling loft-type spaces one might see in New York City.

There were all forms of art being created. Much was traditional, but many artists were working with what appeared to be robots and other machines hooked to computers. Some paintings took on a form that entered dimensions difficult to describe. As one looked at the painting it would start to change and interact with them. An electronic painting would change on the viewer's command, not only in color but scenes and figures as well. It was as if the paintings could sense that the viewer saw something that wasn't there, so it adjusted to that visualization.

The city was full of sculptures in many different sizes and shapes. Some had functions and some didn't. Photography was everywhere. The building dedicated to photography had laboratories where the latest cameras were creating images that were totally lifelike. After taking the image, a process best described as a form of Photoshop was used, except here one would simply think the changes they wanted and it became so.

Cameras were impregnated into fingertips so all that was required was to point and shoot. One's thumb would contact the hand when ready, and the image was taken. This was the same for video because the same camera did both on your command. If images were to be saved, the finger plugged into a reader, and all the images were downloaded and their memory in your finger erased. Images were never reproduced on paper and only viewed electronically. To reproduce them on paper would mean trees would have to be chopped down, and that never happened. Pictures could also be viewed in space in three dimension; something that could never be captured on paper.

If one wanted to review their work outside of the lab they could reload any images they wanted into their camera and play them as holograms that were as true to life as life itself.

Writers worked in a separate part of the city that was very quiet. The buildings were cubes built on top of more cubes. They were all soundproof, and if one wanted to spend an extended period of time on site, the nourishment they needed to survive was pumped into the building with the air. You never had to leave the space until you were done, and you were never interrupted. This was not really a rule in the formal sense—there were no rules here. It was, rather, an understanding that distractions were a writer's worst enemy, so all supported their need for isolation.

Everything was dictated electronically and later downloaded to tablets. Great wisdom from being a scientist or maybe a poet was shared with everyone. Sometimes, spontaneous ideas that could benefit all were shared immediately, but most work was not released until finished. In many cases, this could take quite some time, but in this world, time was forever.

The concept of life was sharing everything no matter what it was, with everyone. Everyone was equal in the eyes of everyone else. Hate, jealousy, and greed did not exist. Everyone had all they needed, and thus only pure love existed on the planet. Perhaps Earth was like this in the beginning, but for some reason that had changed and now it was being destroyed because of it. John knew this and knew he had to do something about it. The way to be was right before his eyes, and he wanted it desperately for Earth. How to get there was being offered by the people of this planet.

He turned to Viktor but did not have to speak. It was clear as they read each other's mind that their mutual determination to succeed had been reinforced.

"Ah, Sirta." Jebumo said as Sirta joined them. "Sirta will accompany you to the next stop which, I am informed by Sirta you should very much enjoy. After, I will join you enroute to our final stop."

"Do you still have your love of surfing?" She asked John as Jebumo disappeared into the sky.

"I do, though I'm afraid I haven't done much for a few years. Viktor is a surfer as well."

"I know, and I think you will both like Lake Nosara. It's a 50 mile wide, 100 mile long artificial lake located between two mountain ranges. The lake surface is flat and calm as glass, as you sailors say, because it is totally protected. Nosara has one purpose; playart water sports."

"Sounds nice, but if it is flat and calm all the time, that kinda limits things like surfing doesn't it?" Viktor asked.

"Not at all, Viktor. Nosara is magical and the ability to create large images on the water while you play is endless." She smiled, then added. "I know you love art too."

"Yes I do, but now I'm really confused." Viktor responded.

"You won't be. Let's go play." She took off, with John and Viktor in hot pursuit.

They flew over more incredible landscape and nourished themselves along the way. Soon, they arrived at what was obviously the lake. There was also a series of what appeared to be giant slides, at least 50 stories high, erected along the most beautiful white sandy beach they had ever seen.

They landed and saw that there were no buildings, just racks containing very unusual looking surfboards and equally unusual looking wetsuits. There were two types of slides. One resembled a giant playground slide and the other had a double loop on the end that eventually shot out flat.

"Now that's what I'd call some serious slides. But what are those things?" Viktor asked, pointing towards a wall full of giant tube looking things.

"Those are a type of magic marker with special grips that make them very secure to hold. They contain the entire color spectrum and with a twist of your thumb, you choose the colors. The surfboards are also capable of ejecting colors by pushing the buttons located on them. You can create any image, in any colors you desire as you surf along."

"Holy cow!" Viktor exclaimed like an excited kid. "Surfing and creating art at the same time. I'm in heaven."

John and Sirta laughed as she continued her explanations. "Now you'll notice that you ride the boards on your knees if you want your hands free to use the markers. Your knees go into the slots on the board and you steer by moving your knees up or down to go left or right."

"And the wetsuits?" John asked.

"You don't need wetsuits on the boards because once aboard, your skin forms small suction cups that will keep you attached. The wetsuits are for those who don't want to use boards or just want to get 'up close and personal'. They are made of a metallic fabric that is very slick because of a membrane that constantly sweats. You can also use the hand markers to create art as well."

"So with that suit, I can go off the slide and skim along the water while I paint." Viktor said, in amazement.

"Yes, except I should point out that after you go through the two loops and exit the slide, you will be traveling 150 miles per hour and your ride will last 30 to 50 miles, depending on how much you dip your markers, which is also the way you steer."

"O.K. I don't need to hear more. The suit is for me to try first." Viktor said as he headed toward the racks.

Sirta laughed and called after him. "Pick up one of the head video cameras. It will show you the action, both front and rear, and will also record your work."

They watched as Viktor suited up, floated to the top of the slide and launched.

The speed was so fast that at first Viktor could hardly hear anything, and he floated as if in a vacuum connected to the earth, but in his mind he was flying. He was amazed at the control he had and drawing on the water was amazing, especially when he saw his creations.

"I propose we try a tandem board so we can ride together," Sirta suggested after they watched Viktor a few minutes.

"Great. Let's do it." John enthusiastically responded.

The surfboard slide went straight down, leveled off, and shot out at a perfect angle to the water at 180 miles per hour. The feeling was breathtaking and pressing the color buttons left beautiful images like a vapor trail airplanes leave. They created art together and seem to be in each other's head to complement each other's color choice without thinking.

"How about a go with the short board on the artificial wave," Sirta suggested after their second ride on the tandem.

They grabbed the 9' 6" boards and headed to the giant wave. He was amazed at how accomplished his grandmother was and how much she loved it. Probably where he got his passion for the sport, he thought. He could remember how she used to encourage him to go to Gilgo Beach to watch the surfers until finally, as she probably planned, he had to do it himself. He had been addicted ever since.

John and Sirta were putting their boards away when Viktor finally showed up.

"I can't imagine anything being more exciting than this water park," Viktor exclaimed.

Sirta laughed. "Well, this is only half of this particular play area." She pointed to the high, rolling mountain on the other side of the valley lake.

"On the other side of the mountain is a ranch called Rando Crib." She looked at John. "It's one of my favorite places. Do you remember our horseback excursions at your father's friend Fred Burner's place in Colorado?"

"Do I ever. We had fantastic times."

"Yes, we did. Well, Rando spent a long period of time on Earth. He married an earthling and bought a big ranch in Virginia. It was a special place, not like the dude ranches. At Rando's ranch, guests were required to interact with the horses for several days during which time a bond between human and horse was formed. Only then could they ride the beautiful trails. It was very popular. His wife enjoyed horses as well, but she also became very involved with her large organic vegetable farm on the grounds. It was called Marigold Farms and her vegetables were free for the picking."

"Wait a minute. He was on Earth? Is he from Plytar?" John asked.

"Oh yes, he is from Plytar. We sometimes send someone to other planets to interact with the beings there. Particularly planets that seem to be in decline."

"But what about the intervention thing Jebumo explained?" Viktor asked.

"Oh, they don't really intervene. Their job is more to assess the beings there."

"So they're like spies." Viktor quickly stated.

"Well no, we don't really regard them as spies. They simply live as one of the indigenous beings and give input to Jebumo or an advisor."

"Sure sounds like spying to me," said Viktor, not dissuaded from his take on the matter.

"I can see from an earthling's perspective that it could be regarded as spying in a sense. I would point out however, that your idea of spying is to gain an advantage over another group by, as you say on Earth, 'staying one step ahead' of the enemy or competitor. Our goal is simply to be informed enough to make an intelligent decision on the need for intervention." She smiled. "There's a big difference."

"Are there others there?" John asked.

Again Sirta smiled. "That's a discussion for another time. For now, we are concerned with playing, so back to Rando Crib." She continued her explanation. "When Rando's wife died, he requested to return to Plytar and asked to start a horse ranch as part of the play area. It's known to all who enjoy it as the Crib. Let's have a look."

With that, she floated up and headed towards the mountain. John and Viktor followed.

They crested the mountain and before them was another magnificent valley, lush and rolling, that seemed to go forever. They learned the ranch was almost one million acres.

They landed near several large, unique barns and followed Sirta down a path covered with flowers that grew up on both sides and met at the top, forming a tunnel of flora.

As the flora tunnel opened, they approached the endless rows of barns, all facing south into open, rolling pastures.

The barns did not have doors because the horses, like all living things on Plytar, were free to come and go as they wished. Since the horses absorbed food and water in the same manner as the beings, there was no waste, so the barns were immaculate. What little dirt came in was sucked away by a system of in-floor type vacuums. There was a constant sound of music that seemed to vibrate in sync with the visitor's heart. The walls seemed alive with music and energy at the same time.

Then, they saw the horses.

Well, Plytar's version of horses.

Certainly they appeared more equine than anything else, but with very distinct, and to John and Viktor, unique features.

The beasts were easily eighteen hands tall with rippling muscles and—no hair.

Their skin looked almost reptilian and glistened as if wet, with several colors shimmering across their bodies. They had four legs attached to lizard like feet with six toes. Protruding out from the top of each front shoulder was a small wing, webbed, perhaps a foot in length. The tail was short and flared into a flat, wide appendage the final two feet. Their neck was massive, and the head was very similar to an earth horse except for a short, stubby, hollow horn-like growth that protruded out just above large, deep black eyes.

"Okay, as an inner city boy, I've never seen many horses, but I think I'd remember if they looked like these dudes," Viktor said.

Sirta laughed. "these wonderful animals were teleported here from a dying planet. They are in their original form, as with all animals brought here, but they are transformed and can communicate. The wings steady them at high speeds, and the tail serves as a rudder. The little horn on their head acts like a sensor to help avoid collisions. They can move very fast."

"Well, if you don't mind, since I've never even been on a horse, I think I'll pass on this." Viktor obviously felt uncomfortable.

"So the guy who has raced every mechanical contraption known to man is balking at a real ride." John chided.

"You know me, John. I like to go fast, but that's when I'm in control and not at the mercy of some strange beast. No offense, boys and girls."

"None taken." One of the horses replied.

"Viktor, I guarantee it will be the ride of your life. As good as the waterpark, I promise." Sirta said.

Viktor still looked doubtful.

"Let me explain a few points that may make you feel better." Sirta approached a horse while several others observed. "First of all, the horse chooses its' rider. Somewhat different than on Earth. After you mount, your inner legs form suction cups that bond with your friends skin. It is impossible to fall off. You ride bareback; no saddle, no reins. Instead, you place your hands on each side of the neck at which time your thoughts sync with his thoughts. You guide the horse by thinking your move. It's translated instantaneously." She smiled mischievously at Viktor.

"And Viktor, while you can ride on the ground, it's far more fun in the air, where your speed can reach 100 miles an hour, and the most amazing acrobatics can be performed. Endless spinning, loop-de-loop, corkscrewing, and of course racing flat out. Some say it's like flying ahead of time and entering a different reality where the colors of the rainbow surround and caress you."

Viktor looked thoughtful.

"I'm in." He said, with a big grin.

They all walked down the rows of horses, and each in turn was picked by one of the magnificent creatures.

Once all riders were aboard, the animals moved slowly into the open, allowing the rider-horse bonding to take place. Sirta and her mount darted into the sky with John and Viktor close behind.

Through thought transference, John heard Sirta. "Figure eight. You're right, I'm left."

They soared out and up in wide arches, passing in the middle and continuing up and out until a perfect 8 was formed like a colorful rainbow.

Viktor charged straight up at blistering speed into a giant loop.

They all merged and were heading for a huge slide, several miles in length, with a series of twists and turns. The riders could sense a rise in excitement from their horses.

As they entered the slides, the animals seemed to become a part of the polished, mirror like surface. There was a constant sound similar to hollow glass having water rubbed over it. The experience gave the illusion of time travel without ever leaving the planet. It was particularly meaningful because they all, beings and horses, were in each other's thoughts sharing the experience.

Regrettably, it was time to leave the lake and rejoin Jebumo. It was truly a fitting end to an amazing tour.

CHAPTER THIRTEEN

THE PLAN

Jebumo had decided the last stop, and the most important one would be the control center for the planet. Here the shield and chambers were monitored and maintained, an absolute necessity because there was still a lot of bad DNA in the universe. While it was Jebumo's mission in life to manage the eradication of bad DNA, a selected group of Plytar beings was likewise chartered to ensure the security of the control center. Plytar had long been engaged in technology sharing with many other planets. This was based on mutual understanding and trust, but in spite of numerous security precautions, there were those who had tried to penetrate the shields with technology theft in mind. The center was very much aware that there were planets plotting to take Plytar by force, which meant devising a means to breach their shield.

For that reason, constant vigilance was critical to ensure the shields remained intact so bad DNA could never infect their planet. This was also where they manufactured the essence used on other planets to convert them to their new beginning and rid them of the bad DNA.

The buildings were all one story and totally automated, requiring only a few engineers to monitor the operations. It was all set in a deep valley surrounded by mountains. The shield was double thick as a matter of precaution. All the buildings were made of clear glass, like membranes, including the ceilings. It seemed counterproductive to have clear ceilings, both John and Viktor were thinking. Their minds were put at ease when Jebumo explained that while you could see out from the inside, a special one-sided layer covering the roof prohibited observation from above, including from deep space.

The entire complex was powered by solar energy with fields of battery membranes used for backup. Air-conditioning was accomplished by a steady stream of water that flowed over, around, and under the building. The water was very cold because it came from aquifers deep beneath the planet that were forced up by natural pressure. Plytar scientists had developed a way of replenishing the aquifers with the same water by drilling a series of holes connected to pipes allowing the water to run off into football-field-size sumps and over several years flow back to the aquifer again. It didn't matter how long it took because the system was always recycling itself and would never run out of water.

They had chosen this spot for the control center because of its unlimited amount of thermal energy. By just tapping the ground, they could unleash all the power they needed. They wanted to be prepared in the event the stars providing the reflective light above them should go dark. Windmill farms were also in place as backup but had never been used.

The ingredients for the essence were synthesized here from small bits of minerals that had been cloned billions of years ago when they were first mined. Knowing they would eventually run out of the minerals, their scientists figured out how to clone them, thus giving them an endless supply. The cloning process was simple and took only a few minutes. Any civilization that had computers could do it as long as their planet had gold, silver, and plant life. With those few resources and Plytar's formula, the essence could be produced.

If a planet had the bad DNA, it usually also had silver and gold which gave birth to greed and left them in need of help. They also found that if these same planets had discovered how to use computers, that usually meant the technology had been abused and things like nuclear weapons were everywhere.

On Earth, for example, the food chain had been tampered with and GMO's were causing cancer at alarming rates. Bees being killed off by the chemical coatings put on seeds would inevitably cause the entire ecological system to collapse.

This was the curse of computers in the wrong hands. Earth had all it needed to clone the essence and the scientists here were eager to share the information and the synthesized procedure. It was agreed that everything needed existed on Earth, so all they had to do was mix the formula according to instructions, and the purification would begin. Plytar had done this countless times for many planets, and it was always successful. The protective shield and two chambers could also be built on Earth by a man like John Klein, who, propelled by the Plytar DNA planted in his body had the resources and determination required,.

The control center tour was complete and, as planned, a meeting with the essence mixing and distribution scientists was convened to discuss how all this would be implemented.

John would to either build several satellites or buy an existing communication company. He would then need to arm the satellites with canisters filled with the essence and develop a way to cause them all to discharge simultaneously.

It was decided the best course of action would be to buy a communications company rather than wait until the satellites were built and put into orbit. He would need to be careful because any move made was always watched by the power brokers who ran the world.

This was going to be a highly visible move by him. The real challenge would be arming the satellites with the canisters. He had to be ready with answers because satellites were not usually tinkered with once they were in orbit. He knew all his moves would be photographed. The government would worry he was arming them with missiles or some other deadly device, and his competitors would worry he was gaining an advantage on them. He worried most about the competitors because they were driven by the dollar.

Without a doubt, this would prove to be his most challenging project ever, and it had to be done in total secrecy. As a cover, he decided he would reveal to the world that he owned the satellites. Simultaneously, he would file the proper paperwork stating he was preparing to do some required maintenance. Public relations announcements touting how the work would also improve the satellites' ability to communicate by adding a new antenna would be released.

Jebumo and the scientists and engineers agreed to all his ideas and were surprised that he had come to such conclusions so quickly. That is exactly how it had worked on other planets and usually the Plytar's had to suggest it.

The grandson of Tesla was continuing his work in ways he never dreamed. Ironically, John should have been an engineer, but he was pushed by his mother to go into business, which ultimately would evolve into funding his greatest engineering ideas.

With the meeting done, and the planet tour completed, it appeared nothing else remained to be accomplished so John asked if they could go back to the PlayArt complex before they returned home. He could see that Viktor was also hoping he would want to, because they had talked about trying Stoned Immaculate and wanted to give it a try. Jebumo agreed and they were off.

Upon arrival at PlayArt, Viktor asked if he could first go into Time Zero while John went into Stoned Immaculate. Time Zero was the round chamber where you stood on a disk in the middle and manipulated images and created music.

It was agreed, so Viktor went to Time Zero, fascinated with the idea of creating new art blended with music. Once he started, he lost all conscious thought of time and space and just lived in the moment. He became so mesmerized by his ability to create that he didn't want to leave, and they had to slowly shut down the experience to get him to stop.

He later said he became so addicted to the experience that he had "time-zeroed-out." Even though he knew he eventually would have to stop, he felt that if he never did, he would have been happy for eternity. Many of the PlayArt experiences could become addictive, so they all had timers on them.

John finished Stoned Immaculate and Viktor followed. They were both speechless and could not fully describe in words how they felt being shot into space at the speed of light. When they calmed down, they both agreed it was an out of body euphoria and could become highly addictive.

With the PlayArt experience fresh in their minds, they returned to the chamber departure point as instructed by Jebumo.

Jebumo suggested they sit down for one final briefing before returning to Earth. With the mission now at such a critical phase, he stressed the importance that all involved have a clear understanding of the finalized plan.

From experience, it was explained that secrecy was important at all levels of the operation. Word had gotten out on other planets, and most of them never evolved. It was important that they not discuss any of their experiences on Plytar because most people would have trouble believing it, and others might think they were crazy. When they returned to Earth they would be exactly as they had been when they left, except for memories of their visit. They needed to develope a timetable and act as fast as possible because as time passed it would become more likely others would discover the plan and sabotage the project.

Jebumo explained in detail how Earth would evolve in a matter of moments and how important this was to him personally as he tried to rid all the universes of the bad DNA. Once Earth activated their shield and built the two chambers, no one would be able to harm them and they would progress at warp speed. The scientists conducted a brief 'refresh' overview on how they were to build the chambers and clone the essence. John told Jebumo he felt comfortable with the directions. The directions were put on a computer memory stick that Jebumo assured them would work on their computer. He pointed out that the stick could not be duplicated or its' contents shared. This was a security necessity, so John would have to brief his people from the stick.

There was nothing left to do. Preparations for their departure were being finalized while Viktor occupied himself with an art hologram. John was being retrospective, allowing all his experiences to float around his mind. He thought of his grandfather, Tesla. What would the man of science think about all this?

"Your head is filled with many thoughts." Sirta had entered to say farewell to her grandson.

"I was thinking about Tesla."

"I know. He was a man very much ahead of his time." Sensing that John wanted to hear more, she continued. "It was not by accident that Tesla was chosen for our seeding." She now had John's full attention.

"He was purposefully selected." John said, more as a statement than a question.

"We were always aware of Tesla. He had such a brilliant mind. You have many of his notes. Did you ever see anything about the possibility of time travel?"

"I did, but he had many notes on quite incredible, but sometimes impossible theories." John laughed. "I wondered if H.G. Wells inspired his thinking, or if it were the other way around."

"He built it."

John sat silent for a moment. "What do you mean, he built it?"

"While working on another project, he discovered how to get large amounts of power from sea water by a type of fusion process. He found that he could concentrate so much power in a relatively small space that he could warp the space-time balance. When he realized this, he started experiments to cause things to travel in time; theoretically to cause objects to go back in time. Because his financial backers were paying him for work on another project, he surreptitiously began work on a machine to test his theory."

"You're telling me he actually built a time machine?" John stammered.

"He built a small model, and after many failed attempts, he sent small objects back in time. He next tried small animals. That too was successful."

"But no one ever heard of this work. How could he keep something like that a secret?"

"Perhaps the question you should ask is 'why did he keep something like that a secret'?" Sirta responded.

"I have a feeling you're about to tell me." John responded.

Sirta smiled. "You could figure it out, but I will tell you. What Tesla discovered was an object, or animal, could be sent back for a period of time that was determined by the power used and the mass of the object being projected. It would then return almost spontaneously. After further adjustments, the object would take more time to return. The next logical step was a larger machine—one that would transport a human. This is when it became clear to us that Telsa was our choice for the seeding."

"Because of his scientific ability." John interjected.

"No, not at all. We had always been aware of his abilities. No, it was something quite different."

Now John was totally confused.

Sirta continued. "Tesla theorized that space-time had a positive or negative leaning; perhaps a curvature. If positive, an intrusion into the past would tend to flatten out as time and history move ahead so that ultimately, things would be pretty much the same as they would have been without the intrusion."

"And if negative?" John asked.

"If negative, would events move further and further away from their original leaning, causing the pattern of time to change." She stopped and watched John.

"Are you saying he became concerned he would alter history?"

"Over several months, he tried to calculate a way to determine whether or not that possibility existed, and to what degree. Finally, he had to acknowledge there was no way to at least reasonably guarantee it would not happen."

"So he abandoned the project."

"He destroyed the machines and locked all his notes away with the hope that science would advance to the point that his concern would be put to rest."

"That's amazing. For a scientist as dedicated to the discipline as he obviously was to abandon the most amazing discovery to date." John said.

"Exactly." Sirta looked at him with a knowing smile.

Suddenly, John realized why his grandfather had been chosen. What Sirta was trying to tell him. "He put mankind, others, before his own interests and desires."

"His sacrifice left no doubt that he was the one." She placed her hand on John's shoulder. "We were right. The proof is before me."

Jebumo and Viktor approached. "It's time." Jebumo said.

John stood and embraced his grandmother. "Thank you."

"We have much time ahead. Goodbye, John."

It was hard for them to say goodbye. Had it been possible, they never would have left Plytar, but their mission was far more important than their individual desires. The joy of watching Earth transform was all the motivation they needed.

They entered the capsule and within moments they were back on Earth.

CHAPTER FOURTEEN
BACK ON EARTH

On their return, John and Viktor looked the same to their colleagues, but they were very different. As much as they tried to contain themselves, their excitement was obvious. The scientists had many questions, and they weren't always happy with the vague answers the two men gave. They recovered from their dilemma quickly as it became clear they had new and exciting challenges before them.

The scientists and engineers were broken into two teams. The first team worked on the capsules and the other, the essence.

The only scientist given enough information to understand everything was the very trusted John Rogers. Others would have only partial knowledge because the essence would be made in three parts by three separate teams. John, with Rogers' concurrence, felt this was vital because once complete, if the essence was released at the wrong time, the entire project would be in serious jeopardy. The final mixing of all three would be done by John and Viktor to add yet another level of security. This was on Viktor's recommendation, and after some discussion, John had agreed. He knew Viktor still had reservations about

John Rogers and John could see no harm in the extra level of security.

The chambers were made in modular form so they could be transported and assembled easily. The defense shield had a tunnel on one end that led to Earth. The only way in and out of Earth was through that tunnel which led directly to the first chamber. The second chamber was connected to the first by a six-inch-thick lead door that only opened from the inside. It was similar to a bank safe with three-inch-thick rods inserted in all four directions. The rods had a backup of additional rods, so the door had to be opened in sequence. This was done to ensure total entry control. No one could ever enter the planet unless they were deemed friendly.

The second chamber had the same type door leading out. If one made it to the second chamber, they would be aware they were going to have their form changed. Once they underwent form change, they could never bring harm to the planet.

Because the true mission had to be done in secrecy, the chambers themselves had to be built in such a way that they could serve several functions, some of which would be known to the world. John decided to spread the idea that his mining company would do related exploration and state-of-the-art weather testing. Why not? Everyone was interested in the global warming phenomenon, so the rumors would be that John was going to get answers.

Even though he believed in global warming, the pretense was that he intended to prove the theory wrong. He chose this course because he knew the people who would sabotage his real mission would love it if someone could prove the "global warming" theory was false. They were many people getting very rich through various endeavors that contributed to the processes that have been linked to accelerating global warning.

In order to pull this off, several buildings needed to be built to house equipment and personnel. The publicized projects received all the approvals needed and John decided not only to build the capsules but all the outbuildings necessary for the project in the future. Because of the ruse created by a phony project, no one questioned what he was doing or how he was doing it. If a rich guy wanted to spend his money in one of the most remote parts of the world, so be it.

There were inspections, but no one had any reason to believe anything was amiss. There were instances when inspectors would point out processes that could potentially cause a permit to be withheld or delayed. Many of those situations seemed to lack logic, as if someone was intentionally throwing a wrench into the process. John personally intervened several times, and by calling in a few favors, the project kept moving. The plan worked perfectly because it could be done out in the open with scores of workers who appeared to be engaged in routine construction activities. On the surface, it looked just like an advanced weather station, and for the most part, it was. Information was shared with NOAA on a regular basis, as well as any other country that wanted it. Nothing was being hidden, at least on the surface, so permit denials were found to be without substance.

Many thought John was crazy wasting millions of dollars at the North Pole, and that was fine with him. The engineers and scientists who worked there had no idea what was really going on. They didn't need to. It was just a weather station and as far as they were concerned, the two capsules were built to protect operators in the event the weather turned nasty.

The capsules were built larger than first planned so they could accommodate the entire crew at the station. This was not a problem as long as the chambers had all the correct hookups and safety that were needed. All that was left to do when the time was right was to attach the capsule with the essence to the ventilation system. This was easily accomplished by adding a Y-valve with an open port and leaving it empty. Engineers were told it might be needed some day if they wanted to add an extra oxygen supply located on the other side of the Y-valve.

John Rogers supervised the building of the North Pole station and returned to the island. Once finished, they could concentrate on the manufacturing and deployment of the essence.

Back on the island, plans were being made to secure the capsules to the satellites. The essence was now ready and had only to be mixed. This would take place in the secrecy of a very secure lab. John and Viktor were the only ones who knew how to mix the three parts. The parts would not be mixed until the last possible moment, and they would need to wear protective suits throughout the mixing process. The entire environment in the lab had to be totally contained so the essence could not be ingested or escape.

After the mixing, the lab would be drenched with water from sprinklers located overhead and in the walls and floors. All the water mixed with cleaning agents would be drained off and filtered seven times. The filters would then be burned in a controlled furnace that further filtered the smoke, and then burned one more time at over one-thousand degrees.

Now that the essence was ready, the final step was getting it to the satellites. This was no easy task, made more difficult because it had to be done in complete secrecy. John knew the world watched every move he made, so the problem was how to deploy a rocket into space and move it from satellite to satellite without causing any commotion.

They couldn't do this under the pretense of maintenance, because the satellites were operating perfectly, and those who monitored satellites would know that. It was finally decided to conceal the essence in a new antenna.

The antenna would also be perfect for releasing the essence and forming the shield. It would be made from two-inch hollow aluminum, drilled a quarter of an inch in a circle at the top. A thin but strong membrane would separate the essence from the tops of the antennas. Once the pump, invented years ago by Tesla, was activated, the membrane would give way and the essence would be released. The antenna would be filled with the essence and then folded so it could be opened later. A trigger mechanism connected to the pump and disguised as a rotating motor would be installed to release the essence.

The entire system could be installed in just a few minutes and was compact enough to allow one man on one flight to do it all. A press release was prepared announcing John's company would be making communication much better with the new antennas, and since John owned the satellites it seemed a normal situation.

Project costs ran high, but John was committed. He thought frequently about the grandfather he cherished. Many of Tesla's inventions found their way into the project and once completed, all John would have to do was flip a switch, and the essence would be released all over the world simultaneously. That would automatically activate the protective shield and make the two capsules operational.

Finally, everything was ready, or so John thought.

CHAPTER FIFTEEN
PLAYING THE GAME

John and Viktor left the island and returned to New York to prepare for the big meeting day. He had confirmed the Russian rocket carrying his private American astronaut had launched successfully, so John was breathing a sigh of relief when the phone rang.

"John Klein," he answered.

"John, we have a problem." John Rogers came directly to the point.

"What kind of problem? I have just confirmed the rocket launched. Don't tell me the Russians want more money again." The deal he had struck with the Russians to let his man join them on their mission so the satellite work could be done had been a painful process.

"No. I wish it were that simple. They say the U.S government has put a hold on the satellite work."

"What! What kind of hold? We had all the clearances. The thing just launched for Christ's sake." John could not believe what he was hearing.

"I'm sorry, John. I just don't know anything else. You need to get involved."

"O.K. If you get any other information, let me know. In the meantime, continue the ground mission as if everything is still a go." He hung up without waiting for a response and pulled up his phone list. He dialed a number and sat back in disbelief.

"Da." Came an answer.

"Vladamir, my friend, I hope you are well." John said in his best negotiating voice.

"John, I was waiting your call. You know about our problem?" the head of Russia's space program asked in broken English.

"Only that it has been put on hold. What I don't know is why or by whom."

"John, I know only I get the word from the top, and they say your government requested hold. You know the politics, our hands tied, my friend. I can do nothing."

"I understand, Vladamir. I'll find out what's going on, but in the meantime, can you keep us on schedule?" John asked, trying to keep his composure.

"Problem also, my friend. I feel so bad. You paid for your work to go first, before our mission, but we have time only to do both. We cannot wait for this to work out. We must now go to our own satellites. Then, if works out, we go to yours. My hands are, how you say it, tied."

"I understand, Vladamir. How much time do I have to get this problem resolved and get us back on schedule?"

"24, maybe 25 hours. No more." The Russian paused. "I will keep everything ready. You fix, call me. This I can do, my friend."

"Thank you, Vladimir, I owe you. I'll get back to you soon."

"You owe me nothing, my friend. Good luck." As Vladimir disconnected, John was again consulting his phone list. He dialed.

"Richard Clark." A pleasant voice answered.

Clark was a senior staffer on capitol hill who had for many years been John's go-to guy for staying up on various issues in the federal arena.

"Rich, John Klein. How you doing?"

"John, so good to hear from you. Heard about your big satellite communications project. Sounds like good stuff."

"Well, Rich it's exciting, except we seem to have a glitch."

"Just heard your guy went up this morning with our Russian friends. They have problems?"

"No problem there, Rich, but if I may just cut to the chase because of time, someone in the government put a hold on our mission. I'd be grateful for anything you might know about it."

"A hold. No, didn't hear anything about that. Can't imagine what that's all about."

"Rich, this is really important. Can you see what you can find out about how this happened, more specifically who caused it to happen?"

"John, you know I'll be happy to. Kinda curious anyway, but I was just about to go into a meeting with the Speaker, so it may be a little while."

"Rich, it's really urgent, and I would very much appreciate it."

"Hold on a moment."

John could hear mumbled voices as Rich was talking to someone.

"One more minute, John. Need to borrow a computer here to check something." Computer noise mixed with other background sounds could be heard. "John, you still there?"

"I'm here, Rich."

He could hear Rich walking. "O.K. John. Looks like the Senate subcommittee on NASA and related stuff had an unscheduled, closed meeting last night. No minutes yet, so I'd have to run down a committee member to find out what happened." Rich said in a hushed voice.

"Is Henry Stalk still the chair of that committee?" John asked about the powerful majority leader who could get anything done if he was so inclined, or if the price was right.

"Yes, he is."

"Is he in town?" John asked.

"Was two hours ago. Saw him coming out of Polinski's office."

"O.K. Rich. One last thing. Can you get a look at the minutes and see if my project was mentioned?"

"Sure, John, but may take a while because they aren't posted yet."

"You see my problem Rich. I need answers quick to get this thing back on track. I'd owe you big." John used the innuendo ace that Capitol Hill people understood all too clearly.

"O.K. John. I'll see what I can do. I think I know someone who should know or be able to find out. I'll call you."

"Thanks, Rich. I won't forget."

John hung the phone up as his blood pressure began to rise. It had to be Stalk. He was the only one on that committee with enough clout to do something like this without proper justification. The question is why? He consulted his extensive phone list yet again and dialed.

"Senator Stalk's office." A pleasant voice answered.

"Good afternoon. John Klein for the senator please."

"Mr. Klein, so nice to hear from you. I'm so sorry, the senator left to see the President about an hour ago."

"I see." John paused. "Please tell the senator I'll be in his office at eight a.m. tomorrow."

"Oh, I don't know Mr. Klein, the senator has a full…"

John cut the secretary off, "Please tell him. And you have a nice day." He hung up.

John searched his mind, looking for possibilities. It had to be someone with the need and the power to do this. Stalk certainly had the power, but why? Someone told him to. But who? Of course, it may not be Stalk. No, short of the President, no one else had the power and the position to act so quickly. But again, why? Certainly, there were competitors who could buy this kind of favor, but that would be almost radical just to influence a communications upgrade.

The ringing cell phone interrupted his thoughts.

"John Klein."

"John, you were right. Stalk called the meeting and the first order of business was a dissertation by him about the concern over all the civilian activity in space these days. He particularly noted that there needed to be more oversight on non-government projects involving satellites. He specifically mentioned your project and the fact that it was being done with the Russians. He got the others to agree to an order stopping all space entry projects until oversight procedures could be put in place. And John, you're definitely not going to like this part."

Rich paused and continued, "He told the others he would call the President and get the O.K. to stop all those already in space on missions unless they were our own government missions. Yours is the only one in that category John."

"Any ideas about the why, Rich?"

"John, you and I both know you have the where-with-all to get that answer a lot faster than I could."

"O.K. Rich, I can't thank you enough, but I'll try. You'll be hearing from me."

"Anytime, John."

John hung up the phone with the confidence he was definitely seeing the right person tomorrow. He had no doubt that Stalk would be there for his visit, contrary to what his secretary had said. Stalk knew some very powerful people, and he also knew that John was one of the most powerful.

He called Viktor, explained what had transpired and asked him to arrange a helicopter and ground transport to D.C. for six a.m.

The next morning as he and Viktor walked up the steep steps of the capitol building, Viktor could see his boss and close friend was in deep thought. They had said little on the short limo ride from the heliport, and Viktor knew that after all they had been through, the chance that it would unravel because of some kind of power play was eating at John.

"How you gonna handle this thing, boss?"

"I'm convinced Stalk caused this. Who put him up to it, I don't know. He won't tell me or acknowledge anyone put him up to it. He's much too politically savvy to do that. No, he'll assume that I know about his meeting and what was said, so I'll get his canned verbiage about the government's concern and it was just an unfortunate coincidence that our project was in the hopper."

He smiled at his friend. "So, my friend, for these next few minutes, I will become like those rich and powerful cats we're trying to change. Sometimes, as they say, you have to play hardball. The bigger question is will he fear me and what I can do more than he would fear breaking the deal with whomever is behind this."

"You know he may have already figured out that those are his options and just not show for this meeting." Viktor stated the obvious.

"No, he'll be here. These guys are all alike. They really think they're invincible. People like Stalk have spoken in political gobbledy-gook for so long, seldom being questioned, that they actually believe what they say, knowing it's bullshit." John laughed. "See, I just did it myself."

"No, I know what you mean. The master politician in the White House does it every time he opens his mouth, and what's more remarkable is the number of people who keep buying it."

"Exactly," John said as they entered the building.

They made their way through security and were greeted by a very attractive woman.

"Mr. Klein, I'm Marge, Senator Stalk's private secretary. The senator asked me to escort you up."

"Of course, Marge, I remember you. And of course you remember Viktor."

They exchanged brief pleasantries and started toward the Senate offices.

"So good of the senator to see me on such short notice." John said to the secretary's back as he shot a quick smile Viktor's way.

"The senator was delighted you called." She said as they entered Stalk's outer office, and Viktor rolled his eyes.

"John, a most pleasant surprise, though a little more notice would have been nice."

The senator said as he offered his hand with his best smile.

Recognizing the manner of his comment, an 'I'm in charge' thing, John quickly replied, "I'm truly sorry about that, senator, but it is quite urgent, and if not resolved, I fear situations could get awful messy." The ground rule was established: "Don't bullshit a bullshitter."

"Sounds ominous. Come in, come in." He glanced at Viktor with his best questioning look.

"You don't mind if Viktor joins us." John said, not waiting for a response as he moved by the senator and took a seat directly in front of his desk while Viktor headed for the senator's silver coffee service on a nearby table.

"John, how's the family?" Stalk said as he settled into the overstuffed chair behind the huge mahogany desk.

John launched into his game plan. "I'm not here to exchange pleasantries, Henry. I need the hold you put on my satellite project lifted. I don't know yet who is behind this, and I know you've made some kind of deal that may be hard to get out of, but trust me, it will be in both of our best interest to do that."

Stalk was not overly surprised. "Now John, I don't know how you know about a classified, closed committee meeting, but however you know, you are treading on illegal ground. I'd be careful."

"Oh, well, allow me to rephrase. If you don't get this changed today, I believe you'd be making a big mistake." John knew he was probably being recorded, so he chose his words carefully. "This project, as announced, will make life easier, and affect the pocketbooks of hundreds of thousands of people, and as I'm sure you are aware, I have announced that I will be providing equipment free to thousands of educational centers around the country so they can take advantage of the enhanced capabilities. They have all been sent letters to that effect."

He stopped and stared at Stalk for a moment. "If you don't fix this today, or provide a valid reason why the government approval was reversed, I will contact all those institutions and their state governors and the news media, whom I'm sure will demand answers."

"Why John, are you threatening a United States Senator?"

"Of course not, Henry, I'm just telling you what will have to be done. I have, after all made promises which currently, I cannot keep."

He leaned forward. "Now, there could be a reason for your action that I'm not familiar with. If there is, please tell me, and if it is valid, the matter is closed."

"You know I can't do that John. The matter is classified."

"As I am sure you are very much aware, my security clearance is the highest granted because of my government contracts, many having to do with the government's satellites, which makes it all the more strange that your committee would cancel my project. You trust me to work on your satellites, but not my own. Doesn't rub, Henry."

"This is different. The Russians are involved."

"Henry, need I remind you that your NASA astronauts are routinely hitching rides with the Russians because we don't have a program anymore."

John sensed that Stalk's dilemma was sinking in. He decided not to push further.

"Well, Henry, I won't take any more of your time. I hope you will reconsider the committee's actions." John stood and headed for the door. The senator remained in his seat, glaring at John. As he and Viktor opened the door, he turned back.

"Oh, almost forgot Henry. You're up for reelection this year, aren't you?"

When Stalk did not respond, John shot him one last look. "Good luck with that Henry." He held Stalk's gaze for a moment longer, then turned and walked through the door.

John and Viktor were silent as they made their way through the building, eventually arriving at the front steps.

"Damn John, I'd say you got his attention. You think it will work?"

Viktor's question was answered six hours later when John received a call that the government had lifted the hold. The mission was back on.

And now, finally with the push of a button, one man would change the world and all its beings forever.

CHAPTER SIXTEEN

REFLECTION

John sat down in his big leather chair, a Remy in one hand and a Cuban in the other. He felt very satisfied as he contemplated what he was about to do. Everything was in place in a project that had taken five years to accomplish. The fact that it had been done in complete secrecy was an accomplishment in itself. He was ready, but was the world ready? He hoped when he met with the most powerful men in the world and explained it properly, especially immortality, they would agree to go along. Soon he would know his answer.

Viktor entered the room and sat down beside him. "Do you feel you're ready?"

"I'm a bit nervous, but after what we both experienced, the decision to proceed is easy. Yes, I'm ready and can't wait to see it happen."

"How much do you trust John Rogers?" Viktor knew he and John trusted each other completely, but though he had no real proof or suspicion regarding John Rogers, he wanted to find out John's feelings.

"Why do you ask?"

Without hesitation, Viktor said, "If I tell you something because you are my best friend and you tell someone else because they also are your best friend, then they tell someone else who once again is their best friend, before you know it, everyone knows. I know you never told anyone, and I never told anyone, but how can we trust John Rogers not to tell anyone?"

John laughed. "He's just like us and totally committed."

"That may be, but he was never transformed like we were. We are true believers, but we saw it, lived it."

"Viktor, I have known John Rogers longer than I've known you. He's been involved with all my top-secret projects and never once has he leaked any information. He's not going to leak this because it was his biggest project to date, and he's worked on it for five years."

"Well," Viktor said, "maybe I'm just being paranoid, but we both know how important secrecy is. Somebody knows something. Why else would they get Stalk to try what he did? And don't forget, there was also that little affair with Rogers and Allatos Stanton. You have to admit that was strange."

"I appreciate your concern Viktor, but if the project was known by others, we would've been shut down long before the launch. That had to be a competitor afraid he was about to lose business. No one would let us get this far if they knew the real purpose and didn't want it to happen."

John could see his longtime friend was not convinced.

"Tell you what. I'll make some phone calls and have some guys do what they do best; check things out."

"Good. I know you're probably right, but we are so close."

"Yes, we are. Just think about it, we can activate it any moment and no one knows but us. Soon, we'll transform the world." He sat back in his chair, dipped the Cuban in his Remy, lit it and took a long draw. He looked at Viktor and smiled.

"I am going to miss these and not smoking a joint ever again, but the trade-off is being high all the time without any stimulants. Never any side effects and never being sick will make up for it." He smiled. "It's funny how all the things we think are important are urgent because we're counting time, but soon we won't ever count time again. If only we could have figured this out sooner. So much time is wasted thinking we're so important and what we do is important.

"I've observed people my entire life, and I've recognized that those who have the least seem to be the happiest. If one doesn't complicate life, one is always happy. I see my son being much happier than me because he's chosen an uncomplicated life. In my life, I didn't think I had a choice, and so many on the planet feel the same way."

John looked thoughtful and continued. "My son is part of a very small minority on the planet who are off the grid and 'get' what life is really all about. They know how to live it to the fullest. They're the ones with the good DNA. I believe the vast majority will never 'get it.' They'll go on with war, greed and corrupt religion; robots to the thoughts of a few and never breaking the cycle. The only way this ends is with the planet either ruined by war or the environment.

"That's why we have to do this thing, Viktor. It's more than immortality; it's about eternal happiness and saving the planet from destruction. The vast majority of those wars were, and still are, religious wars. Religion has torn the world apart because each religion thinks its way is the right way. The Tao actually talks about The Way, and it's the oldest religion.

"Joseph Campbell said all religions are telling the same story, just in different ways. How can it be that they all believe that they are the right religion, and all must follow their thoughts? Greed is killing the planet and destroying the environment at the same time. China doesn't care how many factories they build and uses coal to electrify them. The car companies think more about their stockholders than emissions, which is ridiculous because they're killing those same stockholders by putting excessive pollutants in the air. The human race just doesn't get it and never will. Global warming is a reality that's *still* denied even with all the proof out there to back it up."

John leaned forward and touched Viktor's knee. "We have no choice but to activate the essence and join the other universes that have done the same thing. In time, all the bad DNA will be wiped out and all the shields will be removed. Science will be advanced to the point that we will travel millions of times the speed of light, to worlds and civilizations that have been evolving before time began. We still think in terms of time, but after transformation, there will be no time because everything is as it always has been."

With that, John rose to his feet. He looked around his library at all the books he had read and hoped to read, and thought how grateful he was to his grandfather for inspiring him all these years.

He pulled a volume from the shelf and started talking again, almost as if to himself. "Think of all the stories written about the goodness of man, of unselfish acts of those who truly cared for their fellow man. Many are just stories, but many are true, based on those who, in many cases sacrificed themselves trying to right wrongs. Always, in those cases, there were oppressors. Power brokers who controlled and dictated how things were going to be. Sounds corny, but the classic good versus evil phenomenon seems to have been around forever. Our history has been driven by men who crave power, and once attained, will do anything to keep it.

"Have we always had more bad DNA than good? The phrase 'good guys always lose' comes to mind. In many cases, those who try to change things, who try to right the wrong, have attempted to do so through force. Even in trying to do good, they chose the action of violence. Almost a contradiction in thoughts and intent versus action. There were exceptions. Ghandi comes to mind, though there were others who fought for change for the oppressed peacefully. Were there simply not enough of the good guys to prevent us from being in the state we're in today?"

He turned toward Viktor. "While we were on Plytar, I asked Gonda, the senior advisor, about a Supreme Being, a god. His response was interesting. He said there were thousands of planets with all manner of life forms, and in fact, where they came from, no one really knew. How Plytar came to be was even uncertain. As a scientist, his thoughts were that if there were a Supreme Being with that much power, then the combination of bad and good DNA must have been intentional. For what reason, he would not speculate, but pointed out that his race was cleansed of bad DNA and was now helping others do the same."

John took on a very serious look. "He said he was not sure how Plytar evolved, or in fact how spreading the essence came to be, because to them, it had always been the way it is. You know what he said then?"

"What?" Viktor responded.

"He said, 'Whether or not a supreme being exists can neither be proven or disproven by science, because if such a being exists, he does not do so within the physical universe. Draw your own conclusion.'"

Viktor looked disappointed. "Well, John, to use your favorite expression, 'there you have it'. The question that many believe they know the answer to, one way or the other, is still not answered."

"Touche'." John replied.

"Besides, I think I like it that way." Viktor said. "what we discovered on Plytar was humbling in terms of what we think we know." He paused, and continued, "it's probably a good thing to be reminded on occasion that we don't know very much at all in the whole scheme of things."

John sat down again and looked out the window. "What I do know is that you and I, my friend, are ready to do our part in the scheme of things."

He turned to Viktor. "The time has come. We'll invite all the high rollers to a big party, then lure the big cats to a meeting and tell them what we've been up to."

He laughed.

"Sounds simple enough, but there's always the chance they'll throw us off the roof so our insanity won't spread."

PART III

OUTCOME

CHAPTER SEVENTEEN

BACK ON THE ROOF

John snapped out of his daydream covering five years of reflection about an extraordinary series of events just as Viktor finished his comments.

From the time he had opened this meeting until he turned it over to Viktor, he had tried to read his audience, but at this moment, he wasn't sure which way it was leaning. This was the most important day of his life, and the entire world needed him to be successful. He'd conducted many board meetings over the years, but this one was by far the most important.

Gathered here were the major players who shaped the world. Collectively, they decided everything, and the rest of the world followed. If they wanted to make drugs legal, drugs would be legalized. They owned the media, thus controlling public opinion. With enough well-placed, well-timed stories and editorials, they could get any elected official to do whatever they wanted.

Because so many people, including several here, made huge amounts of money from illegal drugs, they just left things the way they were. That was just one example of how powerful they were. John knew full well who he was dealing with because he had done business with several, and many were rivals. He believed in keeping his enemies close. This meeting would be conducted with that in mind. This was his first rooftop meeting he had conducted under a tent, but it was necessary in order to execute his plan.

John stood and explained everything he'd been doing for the last five years, leaving out a few details better saved for the end of the meeting when he would ask them for their opinions. He hoped they would not think he was crazy. After all, he'd just told them he'd visited another planet where he became thirty years old again, and everyone lived in eternal bliss. He was happy Viktor was there to back him up. He left out what he'd done with his satllites for obvious reasons, and planned to ask them if they would contribute additional funds to finish the project completely.

All were stunned, and many just sat like they were in shock. John had anticipated that reaction and was ready for opposition even though he was promising them eternal life, free from disease and war. These were intelligent people, probably some of the most intelligent on the planet, yet he knew that greed and power had ruled their entire lives, some for many generations.

He also knew that as with most intelligent people in positions of power, they knew all the answers to everything and didn't enjoy people who try to tell them otherwise. They were, likewise, of the 'show me' ilk; 'if I haven't experienced it or seen it, it must not be true'. For them to believe his incredible story would be asking a lot from such a crowd.

John asked around the room if anyone was free of disease, a headache, or pain. He asked if they knew of anyone who was sick among their immediate family or friends. Of course he knew everyone was aware of someone. Many had been very sick or were sick right now, and a couple had terminal cancer, but wouldn't reveal it.

He'd really hoped they would support his idea so was somewhat surprised when it started becoming obvious they didn't, though he shouldn't have been. Throughout Earth's history, intelligent civilizations had always found a way to destroy themselves. These men had had it all for a long time and they were in no rush to share it with the rest of the planet. Some had worked hard for it while others just inherited it. One thing was for sure; no one was going to give it up just like that.

John organized his thoughts and looked around the room. "Who here is happy, really happy?"

A silence came over the room as if they had to think about it. No one answered.

"If you have to think about it, might that suggest that you aren't?"

"Well John, it probably depends on what you mean by the word *happy*," offered one attendee.

"If I need to define it, you should realize you are not happy. Happiness doesn't need to be defined. It's what you are and you know it right away. It's something you feel every day and it's easy to talk about."

Another guest spoke. "Who needs happiness when you have as much power and wealth as we do?"

John laughed politely. "So you define happiness as having money and power even though it doesn't make you happy. Does that make sense? This is the problem with the world. We go along attaching happiness to things that are external, not realizing they don't make us happy. We can only be happy *inside* to be truly happy, and we only do that by living in the *now*, in the moment. You're all fixated on what you'll have next instead of being in the present, grateful for what you already have. The saying, 'it's always better to give than receive' fits perfectly here. We have the ability to give the world another chance. We have the opportunity for true happiness by doing good for all living beings. It's up to every man and woman in this room to save this planet and rid it of its bad DNA."

One of the powerful bankers spoke up. "How can you possibly expect us to believe that we will not need an economy anymore?"

John answered, "First of all, you can't believe that what we have created here in the world is fair. The people sitting here are among those who have 99% of the world's wealth. One percent of the world's people have 110 trillion dollars. That's us. We're the one percent. Maybe you went to college and you worked hard, but do you deserve this much? You're working toward a one-world currency. Why? You don't have enough power? You need more even though it doesn't make you happy? Can't you see how the system is not only failing the 99% but failing the 1% as well? You're blind if you think they will continue to let this happen without a fight. Can't you see the Army turning on you like it has in history for many hundreds of years? I believe happiness can only be achieved when we are all equal and the worship of money—the root of all evil—is eliminated forever.

"Like Bob Dylan said, 'if you have nothing, you've nothing to lose.' This is pure logic." John took a sip of water.

"John, I'm having a difficult time finding rational thought in your suggestion that we basically throw away everything we have built." One of the oil industry moguls stated.

John replied, "Not throwing away. Just changing priorities; looking at the bigger good.

"I'm considered the richest man in the world and maybe the most powerful, and though some of you would debate that, you *do* understand what I mean. Most of you can relate to what I'm about to say. How many days have you been miserable because a project got caught up in government red tape or a partner stole money or secrets from you? You all know what I'm talking about. The majority of our time is spent in trying to resolve or negotiate conflict. Conflict is not fun and it is not pleasurable. And we do it, day after day, slaves to a system we have created and foster. This begs the question, 'what went wrong and how do we fix it?'"

"John, I can't argue that you may in fact be the most powerful man in the world, which begs the question, 'what's in it for you?'" a well-known internet guru asked.

John paused and looked around. He suddenly felt very tired. That always seemed to be the question with powerful people; 'what's in it for me'. "As I speak to you today, every aspect of the human condition is falling apart. It started accelerating three decades ago and has increased under every presidential administration since then, but it started long before that. Here we are sitting around this table, the very ones largely responsible for this condition which we can now change, and we're debating why we should. Does anyone think maybe we've lost our way? With just a few billion more dollars, this plan to change things could become operational."

John suggested a half-hour break to give everyone time to talk with each other or perhaps to reflect on his invitation. He also needed a chance to regroup.

Viktor approached John. "How do you think it's going?"

"I guess I should've expected this. We know who we're dealing with. If this were any other group of people, they would have jumped at this opportunity. These men think they have more to lose than to gain, but it really bothers me that they're so blind with power and money that they can't get a grip on what is really important like health and immortality for all. They won't trade what they have now for a better condition. This shows you how power corrupts even the mind and good reason." He smiled.

"The last thoughts these people will have before they transform will be these thoughts of losing their power, but soon it won't be important because they will all want to rid the rest of the universes of the bad DNA. The more beings we have doing it, the faster it will happen."

When the break was over, John decided to cut to the chase as he addressed them again. "I'm asking you to help change the world. I'd like to see how far we have come in our meeting today. Please raise your hand if you're with me."

Only the Vice President raised his hand. John nodded. The vice president was not a rich man and knew that his power of office would be short-lived. John appealed to them again. This time, he was more forceful.

"I've told you that both Viktor and I have traveled through time and space. We were transformed into a being that was thirty years old. Who among you would not want to be thirty again and live for all time at that age? Never sick, never at war. This is *real* my friends, and when it's all over, you'll be the ones who are revered for causing it to happen." He stopped and looked around. 'One last appeal he thought to himself.'

"Everything we see and know is temporary and the Earth has been so damaged by us that we cannot fix it without help. That help is being offered. We can't take our power or money to the grave and be reborn. We die and that is it. Most of our money will be wasted and we won't have any control over it anyway, even though we set up those irreversible trusts. I've seen them broken time after time. My mother broke up my grandfather's so I know what I'm talking about. The fact that I even need to have this conversation with you is amazing to me."

Ronald Murdocke, a global media and communications king cleared his throat. At 86 years of age, he was still a giant in the financial arena.

"Now John, I'm not a young man, so I'm open to any possibility to grab a few more years."

There was respectful laughter.

"But John, for goodness sake, what you've said you experienced is just too incredible to believe. And, really John, isn't this bliss where everyone is equal that you envision just another form of communism where nobody owns anything and big brother doles out the crumbs."

More mumbling in the crowd. Some voicing agreement.

"Not at all, Ronald." John took on a thoughtful expression. "You are right that communism is a theory advocating the elimination of private property. I see that what I've described sounds similar in some respects. Communism has never worked because in that system goods are owned in common and are available to everyone

162

as needed. The system has a major flaw." He looked thoughtful again.

"That totalitarian system of government depends on an authoritarian party, all powerful, that controls state-owned means of production in an aim to establish a stateless society. That could not be more different from what I've seen and what I'm advocating to save our earth."

"Well, again John. How is it so different?" Murdocke responded.

"For one thing, material possessions, as we know them won't exist. Likewise, there is no government, totalitarian, democratic, or otherwise. There's no need for one because everyone is equal, and rather than pursuing material gains, they live to think, create, play, engage in discussion. There is no competition because there's nothing to compete for. Unlike our society, where only winners matter, and our kids start learning at birth to get what you want, you compete." He paused.

"Look where that has gotten us. Why would you need any form of government when there are no rules or laws to be enforced and no 'things' to be controlled by the volumes of commerce regulations we have now? How could you ever have a fair and equable system with what we have now? A congress with power and no term limits so their biases and interests are perpetuated as long as they have the money to get re-elected every few years. The same is true of positions appointed for life, like judges, whose leanings dictate every phase of life."

John looked directly at Murdocke. "No, Ronald, what I am talking about is very different. I know it's hard to grasp, but please, open your mind. Look beyond 'impossible' simply because you've never seen such a system. I'm telling you it exists."

It had become very quiet. The slight humming of air conditioner units outside sounded like a freight train. John realized there was not much more he could say. He made one last effort.

"Think about your children, the world's children. Look around at what you're leaving them. Would you want to start out in a world that's falling apart and a society so full of distrust we won't even help an old lady being robbed on the street. Yes, change is scary, but what we're talking about here has nothing to do with money or power, neither of which has given you bliss. We're talking about bliss forever, and you're still hesitating.

"Even if you can't fully accept what I have told you about the help, the opportunity that's being offered to us, isn't it worth taking a chance on?"

The man known as the king of wall street stood and started to speak. "John, with all due respect, we have our own plans for immortality. Stem cell research has advanced so much that we think it is possible right now for humans to live a few hundred years, and by the time they might have expired, we believe it will be perfected so that you can live forever."

He gestured around the room. "While you were busy building your antenna and traveling to who knows where, we've been secretly perfecting stem cell research in our own laboratory away from the press and government. We never approached you because quite frankly we've always thought you a bit of a bleeding heart liberal." There were a few murmurs around the table as he continued.

"Charities you've supported over the years were not the ones we would've chosen. We knew that if we told you our plans to keep the serum to ourselves and not share with the rest of the world, you would have balked. We didn't need

164

your blessing then and we don't need it now." He laughed and threw his hands up.

"So now you come to us with this crazy idea that all of mankind should be equal and we just flat don't agree with it. We also think it would be quite boring without a good war every once in a while to thin down the less mentally equipped. With the new technologies that are being developed we will clean up the environment before it gets out of hand. Right now we're having too much fun playing with it. We're rearranging the weather on the planet, and when we're done the Northeast will resemble Florida's weather."

He paused and stared at John for effect. "You've been out of it my friend. Yes, you were right about the One World Currency. We will rule the world, but first we have to bring them to their knees, so they come begging to us to feed them. You think there will be problems with the military because you believe they'll side with the people. That may be true, but who needs the military? We already have in place contractors who are doing a lot of the military's work, and they'll always be beholding to us. If that isn't enough, we've also developed robots, and you already know about drones. We'll have thousands of them ready to attack any one or any group that tries to defy us.

" Never in the history of the world has communication from human to human been so easily monitored. Every move they make against us will have a swift and punishing outcome. If they want to eat, they'll have to obey. This is global my friend. Hitler tried to do it and failed because the technology wasn't there. Well, we have the technology to rule the world and we will. If you're a good citizen, you'll be given food and a place to live. You'll only be allowed to have two children or less. Those who are weak and can't contribute to society will be eliminated. The welfare state will come to an end. Most of the work in the future will be done by robots anyway, so we need to remove those who are nothing more than a drain on everyone else."

John jumped out of his chair. "Have you all gone mad, or is someone among you related to Hitler?"

"Sit down, John!" mister Wall Street commanded.

"We listened to your presentation for hours, so now you listen to us. We've always been creating the future for the world today. We've much better tools than before and it wouldn't make sense for us to share that with everyone. We learned over the years by keeping our group small, we guarantee success. What you've done today is forced us to share some of this with people who are not part of our group." He glanced around. "I'm sorry to say we don't want any new partners. So some of you will be eliminated."

The Vice President jumped up and said, "Are you crazy? You can't just eliminate the Vice President of the United States!"

"Yes, we can. We've taken out presidents and kings all over the world. In fact, we eliminated a president here, so make no mistake; you can easily be done away with. How much did you know about what we were working on?" He paused, but there was no response.

"Let me answer for you; *nothing*. We've been running the world for a very long time, and some of you political fools still believe you have the power. A few of your presidents were aware of us because we like them and the way they thought. Some actually still work with and for us." He turned back to face John.

" So John, we are *not* with you."

John stood. It was now clear who had tried to stop his satellite work. "I knew this might happen, but I confess I had no idea you would be so well-prepared to reject the project. What you're proposing is really the opposite of what I am proposing, but did you really think I called you all together today because I needed your money to complete the project? It's already in place and ready to be activated."

One of those anonymous, powerful people the world never hears about stood and pointed a gun at John. Another drew a gun and aimed at Viktor.

Almost simultaneously, four men appeared, each holding machine pistols. They spread around the group perimeter, effectively surrounding all participants.

"John, what a fool you are. Did you really think you could keep all this from us for five years?" He shook his head in mock sympathy." We are very disappointed in you. This is part of the reason we chose not to inform you about what we were doing.

" Your confidant, John Rogers, has been working for us for years. Why do you think the Chinese have been able to copy all your inventions so quickly? We've made Rogers a billionaire and he answers to us. We've been aware of every move you've made. You think today you're going to activate your satellites and change the world, but what you don't know is that we have an antidote." He laughed again. "Not that I really believe your bullshit story anyway, but it never hurts to be prepared."

He looked at Viktor. "You were right about Rogers."

John was stunned, but he didn't believe they had an antidote and were probably bluffing. They probably suspected he had a backup trigger, explaining their need for guns. John knew at this point he was going to die along with Viktor on the rooftop of his building. Not a major surprise when one considered who he was dealing with.

He was surprised and disappointed by how he had been fooled by John Rogers all those years. When Viktor told him he was concerned about Rogers, he looked into it, but nothing turned up and he had been quite relieved. Yet, he always knew the only person he could totally trust was Viktor, so a few secrets had been kept from Rogers, and that was proving to be very important.

John asked if he could speak one last time. He held his hands in front of him, the right over his left wrist, covering his watch. The Wall Street king inclined his head in agreement.

"I listened carefully to what you've said and how you see the world. It's obvious that we do not share the same vision. You're looking at more of the same. You think new technologies will keep you in power, help you to live forever, and give you infinite control. That's never worked in the history of this planet or probably any other planet in any universe when attaining power is the motivation.

" I know from notes that my grandfather knew this. His dream was to build a power source that could communicate with other, more advanced civilizations because he knew time was running out. He understood that *everything is*, and he wanted to find a race who could bring that to earth. Yes, we're advanced, but as long as there are people like you on Earth we will *never* truly advance.

" You've left out peace and love. Nothing in your remarks even mentions it. In fact, you talk about war as a good thing and elimination of the poor and oppressed as necessary. You fail to understand human nature and the desire to be free. Those you hold down will fight you and everyone will ultimately die. My vision for beings to be as one does work because I've seen it with my own eyes."

He paused and looked around. "Today you will kill me and others around this table. When does the killing stop? I'll tell you. It never stops until everyone is dead and the planet no longer exists. This is not so far-fetched. There are many nuclear weapons that are not accounted for since the breakup of Russia. I believe we'll always have rebels and just as you believe technology will keep you in power, it will also destroy you.

"Think of this. You were able to buy John Rogers. In time, someone will buy someone close to *you*. Greed has always worked that way. In a thousand years, everything you see here today will be gone. I beg you to work *with* me, not against me, and let's change the world together."

What the group didn't know was that Viktor had convinced John that certain things should never be shared with anyone else. This was probably the most important decision they had ever made. They had changed the code to trigger the essence, and they had never let Rogers know the exact proportions that were in the formula. That's why John knew they didn't have an antidote. He and Viktor had also installed a canister containing the essence under the conference table. Once activated, under the small area of the tent, it would take effect immediately.

The ring leader waved his pistol. "While we've been on this roof listening to your pipedream, a specially equipped rocket was launched. It will be removing all your antennas in the next few hours." He shot John a smug look. "You were able to get to that whimp on the hill we bought and get them up there, but I don't think you'll be intervening this time.

" We like what you did at the North Pole so we'll keep it a weather station. We see a nice contract coming from that effort. Unfortunately, the only way we can deal with your island is to bomb it and kill everyone who works there. Your secret must remain a secret to the world, so no one can be left alive. You did an excellent job keeping your projects secret and we thank you for that."

John glanced at some of the event staff, still performing various duties.

The speaker smiled. "Sorry John, but all the staff working here today works for us. As you can see, we've thought about everything. Your mistake was to think you could keep something of this magnitude from us, and now you're going to pay the price."

With that, the two ringleaders simultaneously shot John and Viktor while the other four gunmen sprayed the crowd with their automatic pistols, though it appeared they knew who to shoot and who not to. As several tried to flee and others dove for cover, Viktor managed to pull his Beretta and began exchanging fire with the shooters.

John's hand had remained in place, covering the crystal of his watch. With Viktor's help, as a final precaution, he had built an essence canister trigger that was concealed in his watch. All he had to do was depress the crystal and the activation would start. At the moment he realized he was about to be shot, he activated the canister.

At that precise moment, all the satellites simultaneously started spraying the essence. The canister in the tent had been positioned because he knew he would have enemies in the room who probably would do all they could to stop him. These were, after all, men who had assassinated many others who had disagreed with them or would not follow their lead. The essence would save John and Viktor and the others if they breathed it in before they died. Everything went according to plan.

John and Viktor survived, and watched in fascination as the transformation began. They felt a combination of elation to be alive and amazement that the essence worked exactly as Jebumo said it would. Deep down inside, they had known it would, but to actually see it happen was uniquely remarkable.

CHAPTER EIGHTTEEN
THE TRANSFORMATION

The scene in the tent was mass confusion before everyone settled down. Many struggled right to the end to maintain the being they once were, but once they made the transformation, all they once were was gone, purged from their DNA.

John and Viktor watched their bullet wounds evaporate, leaving no evidence of injury. John had activated just in time so they could both survive. They were among untold numbers of people who were on the brink of death around the world but were saved when the essence was released.

Unfortunately, those who had already died could not be brought back to life immediately. It would be necessary to first obtain DNA from those already passed and then begin the process that would eventuality bring them back.

Jebumo had decided to allow Earth's transformed scientists to work that problem with Plytar scientist guidance. They could then help with other universes. When the dead did come back into the atmosphere, they would automatically become new beings.

The monitors John had installed were full of images from around the world showing the transformation. No person was unaffected. Soldiers shed their uniforms and dropped their guns as military operations ended around the world. The soldiers were now armed with seeds and immediately started planting for the new nourishment. They knew exactly what to do because of a preplanned thought transference process put in place by Plytar's scientist's as the essence was released.

Hospitals and nursing homes were abandoned as patients walked out in perfect health, now thirty years old again. There was no longer a need for doctors, nurses, dentists, physiologists or anyone else in the health field. Those professionals, like so many others, could now devote themselves to just being. Never being ill and therefore never fretting over the complicated world of health insurance was a major transformation benefit. Health insurance would never be an issue again.

Paperwork of all kind ceased to exist. With no need for money, the entire financial system closed down. Everyone was equal — no class wars. All civil works projects were stopped and civil servants joined the military in planting.

The practice of all religions stopped and all religious buildings were abandoned. No one was confused as to what to do, and they didn't need any organizers. The political organizations including kings and queens were abandoned. Since everyone was now equal, no formal governments were needed. Everyone would share everything with everyone else.

Treasury Department printing presses stopped because money had become irrelevant. There was no more media or Internet since everything you needed to know you knew, and there was no longer a need for more information relating to everyday living. People now lived their lives on instincts, and they were always right. Information to satisfy curiosity or to aid in research was being compiled in centers that would replace traditional libraries. Knowledge could be acquired with the touch of a finger and computer to mind downloading.

Among the most active transformed were the scientists and artists. The scientists immediately started working on new antennas and bringing the dead back to life. The artists were bringing joy to the landscape by reforming everything in sight. Before, thousands of these artists had worked a variety of jobs out of necessity. Now, their time could be devoted to creating. Because there was no need for many of the buildings, they were transformed into PlayArt complexes.

To clean the seascape, all motorboats were drained of their fuel and taken out to sea and sunk where they would become reefs for sea life. People did not need them anymore, and they just took up space. The same was true for cars and trucks. Most went down with the ships, and the rest were put in the desert for artist's to create new works.

Nuclear power plants shut down immediately, along with any power producing plants that were polluting the planet. Sun, wind, and ocean waves would now supply energy. Because very little energy would now be necessary, everything currently in place was all that would be required. With the sun shining twenty-four hours a day and vehicle type transportation gone, the only energy needed was for the scientists and artists. New power-generating ideas were already being discussed for the future. The Earth has many hotspots where energy could be tapped. Pure quartz could also be used now that scientists could apply more time to the processes.

Soon the landscape and seascape would become clean of the clutter of the old forms of transportation. Trains were dismantled but the tracks were kept in place because great ideas for their use were being developed for PlayArt.

No one needed to fly anymore. When airplanes flew into the essence, it went into the air intakes and everyone was transformed. All airplanes and helicopters headed for the nearest airport. Once there, all passengers deplaned and left their baggage behind. Too bad George Carlin wasn't on hand to see people give up all their stuff. The planes were dismantled, and the wings were used for tables. The fuselages were taken by the PlayArt people, and they designed a ride down Niagara Falls.

A silence came over the land that was comparable to the time before transportation advanced from walking to vehicles. The wheel was no longer necessary and everything, now motorless and wheelless, could be transported in silence. The calm was felt by everyone and enhanced their life experience.

No one needed to shop, so all the shopping centers and malls closed. Bridges were removed because they ruined the natural flow of the land and no longer had a purpose. Cities with their tall buildings remained but were unoccupied because no beings had a need to be there anymore. The buildings would ultimately be used for science, art, and PlayArt.

No one lived any place in particular. Earth was for everyone. All businesses and manufacturing closed. All forms of mail stopped since beings could now communicate with each other at will, telepathically. It was simple; you just thought of who you wanted to talk to and communicated. The need to communicate was limited in the New World because everything was spontaneous.

All beings went about their lives without planned direction because everyone instinctively knew what to do. The animals, both on the water and in the sea, changed immediately. Their aggression to each other and all living things simply vanished. Lions and tigers were more like pets. They, and every being on the planet, could communicate through their mind and thoughts.

Amusement parks like Disney World were kept and modified into PlayArt complexes. All PlayArt museums would become extremely popular and expanding them became a top priority.

When the shield went up, the doors to the double chambers were left open so all the bad air in the planet could escape, and the atmosphere adjusted to seventy-seven degrees at seventy-five percent humidity. Now, the sun shone all over the planet all day long and the shield was able to capture the sun's rays wherever it was. It bounced and reflected the rays so the entire planet was bathed in sunshine twenty-four hours a day and would remain that way every day throughout time.

The atmosphere was the same wherever you went, and now the problem of water shortages ceased to exist. This was possible because all being's membranes took in all the water needed and only what was needed. The same was true for food, so no waste existed. The process was similar to that of some trees and plants that existed before the transformation. This also meant there was no more garbage, so dumps were quickly covered and abandoned. They would in time become part of the natural landscape once again.

The fields were planted and instantaneously started to grow food. After transformation each being had plenty of energy to sustain themselves for days as the food was being readied. Oil was not needed, so all the oil fields were shut down. Anything at all that had to do with pollution just stopped existing.

Even though wheels were not necessary, playing was an important part of everyday life. Non-motorized vehicles became very popular, especially bicycles. Mountain bikes were the most popular and beings would spend much of their time riding them. Skiing was very popular, especially since lifts were not necessary—you skied down and floated back up. Power boats were gone but sailing was still enjoyed. Boats of all sizes could be seen sailing on the waters all over the planet.

An added benefit for all beings was that they could remember their old life so they could compare it to their new. The harder their life had been the more joy they experienced. The fact that they could be whatever they wanted for however long they wanted caused a few to change immediately. Others wanted to just take it all in as the marvel of the new life on earth settled in. All agreed this must be heaven.

In time, the old memories would simply go away, and future generations would know only what now existed; Everything Is.

Back at the tent, the formal meeting was history, but the participants were lingering, talking amongst themselves and looking at the monitors as the world transformed. John and Viktor, like everyone else, recovered very quickly. It was as if nothing had ever happened! No one spoke for a while because everything was much too overwhelming. Finally, through his mind, John spoke.

"Is everyone okay?"

His words were met with broad smiles around the room. A former real estate tycoon turned from a monitor and spoke.

"To try to put my feelings into words is very difficult. I feel my old self and my new self as one. I remember everything, yet it has no meaning. I remember when it had meaning so I know the difference. I only wish that all those years we thought that what we did was so important, we had realized just how unimportant it was."

There were murmurs of agreement around the room as the Vice President walked over and put his hand on John's shoulder. " John, thank you for doing this and especially your decision to have this meeting. You didn't have to risk your life. You could've pulled this off without us but I see the wisdom of your actions. We all needed to remember the decisions we were going to make. Now, we truly understand the difference as we go forward. I am sure I speak for most, if not all of us, that we want to rid the other universes of the bad DNA and will do all we can to that end."

All the others nodded in agreement. They were all feeling true bliss for the first time in their lives with the knowledge that it was real bliss because they could remember the way they were before. Being the most powerful people in the world was not what it seemed. To think you can control power when you can't results in many of your actions having negative effects on people. As hard as you try to deal with that, it haunts you to some extent, and bliss is only felt for very short moments at a time. Now, after transformation, bliss is felt all the time by everyone, and the feeling becomes magnified.

After several hours of watching the video monitors, they decided to greet the other beings. Instead of taking the elevator down, they just stepped off the roof and slowly descended to the street. The other beings were all walking around as if they were in a trance. This condition would last for a short period of time until their new being could adjust completely. The memories of their past life needed time to leave the uppermost regions of their conscious mind. No one felt any pain or discomfort while this was going on, and it was very necessary because they might need a defense against it someday.

John watched as the others from the meeting began interacting with those around them. His thoughts as an observer were clear, but images from the past seemed foggy.

"What you are feeling is very normal."

He turned to see Allatos.

"Allatos, why are you....I thought you were on the island," John, confused, stammered.

"I am wherever I wish to be, a capability all of you will enjoy soon."

Suddenly, everything was clear to John. The discussion with Sirta at Rando Crib on Plytar, Allatos making him aware of the teleportor problem.

"You're from Plytar." John stated.

"I am, and you have done well."

"But why didn't you tell me when we spoke on the island?"

"It was not necessary, and you did not need distractions." Allatos stated in a very matter of fact manner.

"But John Rogers could have sabotaged the entire project." John pointed out.

"That is why I was sent here, and it is the past, which is no longer important to us. After the adjustment period, all thoughts of the past will have no relevance to the present because everyone lives in the Now. This very powerful living-in-the-moment is a significant reason for the bliss everyone now feels.

"True, you are all healthy, both mentally and physically, which is what most beings feel when they are thirty. But, for the most part, as a planet, you do not live in the moment. You never fully realized the past was gone, and you couldn't do a thing about it, and the future was the same. Bliss exists now because all you have is the present moment. When there is no past or future to rule you, you are free to live life to the fullest."

"The state of bliss we saw on Plytar." John recalled.

"Yes, and as the Transformation runs its' course, the absence of endless desires, another burden, is lifted off your shoulders. The freedom of not wanting or seeking pleasure outside of yourself. Going inward as a way of being outward becomes evident to all other beings who in turn embrace this energy and make it their own. In the end, we are a mirror to all those around us. So all these beings are now reflecting bliss to each other and the true definition of being blissful is being felt everywhere. The unknown has become insignificant until it is relevant and it becomes relevant only when it becomes the now."

John interjected, "So the state of fear most of us previously lived in because of the unknown is disappearing.

The old saying, 'the only thing to fear is truly fear itself', something almost impossible to grasp before the transformation, is no longer valid."

"Correct. Now, fear does not exist, so you can all do or be anything you desire because fear is no longer an obstacle." Allatos replied.

"Will you now return to Plytar?" John asked.

"No, Jebumo asked me to stay long enough to assist in the shield development." He paused, then continued, "That has now become a more urgent priority."

"Why more urgent?"

"Soon, you will be fully briefed by Jubumo. For now, you need only be aware that a hostile planet has shown an interest in Earth. We believe they have enlisted the services of the Cantaureans, a space warrior clan who does others' dirty work."

"Are they here? What shall we do?"

"They are not here. So far, we believe the Cantaureans are using only unmanned craft to observe. These ships are equipped with artificial intelligence and engage in information gathering. It is possible their employers may now lose interest since the Transformation has started. But they know, as you must now understand, that not all beings always transform. Some DNA is so corrupt, its' host will resist for a long period of time. That means they are susceptible to the influence of those who would change or destroy us. That is why the shield has become vital. It is important you understand this."

"I understand."

"Good. Now, I need to return to the island and get to work. I'll see you soon, but in the meantime, go, enjoy your friends. Watch the transformation and your new world unfold. Our minds will stay linked so you can envision all that is to happen."

With that, Allatos floated away.

John could indeed see or sense all that lay ahead.

The buildings were emptying of beings and the streets were filled. Some instinctively started to transport themselves, and the sky became full of beings going in all directions. Before long, the city was empty and the first places many wanted to go were PlayArt museums, skiing, sailing, mountain bike trails, amusement parks; anything that was play oriented.

It was truly analogous to Viktor's story about children getting out without parents for the first time and feeling the exuberance of being free.

The PlayArt movement had been underway for quite some time, but the difference now was that people had time to enjoy it. The city had no food so they needed to go to the countryside to allow their membrane to take in nutrients within twenty-four hours. There was plenty for everyone because all plants gave up something of value to the beings.

Water would never be an issue with seventy-five percent humidity. They just absorbed all they needed from the atmosphere.

Some began to have sex and it didn't matter with whom or how many, where or when. Without inhibitions, one felt free from guilt for being a being. Most of the sex happened in the air as one would attract another as they were passing by. A loving embrace could become contagious and several hundred might join in at the same time. Love was all around. Everywhere you looked you felt it. The freedom to express it was felt naturally by all and not encumbered by how you were brought up or dictated by past relationships. Love was the mantra that all lived by.

Every being remembered their past, but it had nothing to do with the present. It just made the present more wonderful. Instead of dragging you down, it lifted you up and caused you to appreciate the now. Beings would break into song at a moment's notice, and soon hundreds of thousands would be singing together. The sound would roll over the land and extend for miles. If you heard it, you felt yourself compelled to sing and join the choir of voices. They were not singing songs but rather were rolling out notes like Ella Fitzgerald. Going from high to low in such a way that the body felt bathed by the sound. It had the ability to make you feel weak and strong at the same time. The joy of so many voices gathered together and singing as one was almost overwhelming. This happened above ground, but like a school of fish they would come together and reach high notes and then slowly move apart into the low notes and then back again.

Occasionally, like birds that fly in formation, a leader would be at the point. All the other beings would follow as they flew through the sky and the notes would go from high to low and back again. So the planet was always serenaded with music that was both soothing and exciting. No one ever got tired because the volume was always perfect. If you wanted to be in total silence you could fold a part of your ear that removed all sound.

Once the initial excitement abated, groups started to form to do different tasks. Parts of the earth that had never been farmed came to life with an ever abundance of all that would ever be needed.

PlayArt centers were being developed in spaces that were previously used for manufacturing, along with airplane hangars and other large structures. The scientists already had laboratories that were used by drug manufacturers to do their design and development work. In fact, the earth had all the infrastructure in place for everything that was needed.

Skiing was initially limited to areas where energy from the ground could be cooled and made into man-made snow. Since the planet was a constant seventy-five degrees, snow-making without pollution needed to be perfected. A gentle breeze was always blowing and the Caribbean had all the wind necessary for sailing.

Some beings decided to be transformed into fish, birds, and other animals and did so immediately.

Artists could be seen transforming the landscape into giant works of art. Soon no building existed without a mural painted on it. Sculptures were being made from everything left behind when the factories closed. Everywhere you went, art was taking place on both a small and grand scale. The Arts and Crafts movement that William Morris developed in the eighteenth century was alive and well. If he was alive, he would have been pleased that humanity finally got it right. Everything was made by hand with whatever hand tools were necessary to perform the work. The only thing people craved was art and more art. That was the best way for them to create and express themselves, and since they had all the time they needed, the works were amazing in size and form.

Remember, in the New World you could be anything you wanted for as long as you wanted. Once fields around the globe were planted, nothing was ever needed again. The food just kept regenerating itself and never needed any tending. So art, science, and play was the primary pastime enjoyed by all.

Once you felt you wanted to do something else, you simply did it. There was no competition, no prize to win; no one judged you or your work. They simply appreciated it with you. Most of all, the gift of total bliss is that you never need dwell on the horrors of the former Earth or feel guilty for your role in it. None of this was realistic in the old world the way it had been organized.

***

John pulled Viktor to his side and thanked him. He knew that had Viktor not alerted him to the problems with John Rogers, the plan may have failed. He never saw that betrayal coming. Part of the reason was because John lived a charmed life, while Viktor was a rebel and street fighter most of his life. John went to all the best schools, which in some ways was a detriment because places like Harvard teach you how to make money but not how to go to war and sniff out an enemy. All that gentleman crap is sometimes a mask for a knife in your back. They were good at that but lacking in street smarts.

Neither one of them was tired, yet it seemed they should be after what they had gone through in the last five years. They knew the men on the island would quickly forgive them for pushing so hard once they were transformed and didn't need money anymore. John Rogers was a brilliant scientist and he immediately found his way and started work on improving the antenna. They never spoke about how he turned on them because it was no longer important.Truly, making the world a better place was on everyone's mind.

EPILOGUE

For years I have studied the problems of the world. While teaching graduate school at Long Island University, I was amazed just how little the students knew about what was really going on. Their only source was newspapers and television. Most were surprised when I told them I hadn't watched television in years. They also had never been taught that if they wanted to become productive administrators, they had to center themselves. In those days the Tao was relatively new. I was lucky that Claude Sacks was a friend and Tao master.

The Tao tells us not to live in extremes but in the middle of both energies. Being balanced at all times is the secret of happy and fulfilled life. This, blended with proper eating, is the formula for success in whatever you do.

It is not always easy to think positive all of the time, but what choice do we have? I believe that being optimistic, living without fear, living in the now, is spreading all over the world. We have ways of educating ourselves and the public like never before.

The Internet is changing the world, but we are running out of time. What we have to do is harness its power and put it to positive use. If the entire world were connected, it would rise up as one voice against the people who actually control everything.This is already happening because the information revolution is in full swing. The key is sharing, but the current situation is the opposite of that

If you want to sell something, and I am not only talking about cars, social marketing has become the way to get the word and ideas out. You can reach millions of people in what previously took months in a few hours. Bank of America had to change its policy of charging five dollars every time you used your debit card because it went viral on the Internet. If only we realize just how powerful we are and take control. All big businesses need cash flow or they go out of business. All you have to do is interrupt their cash flow by not buying whatever they are selling, and they will give in.

Almost every politician becomes addicted to the handshake and the attention they get. I am good friends with a gentleman who held political office for many years. I was with him when he lost a primary. He was in shock for a very long time. I worked in the field of addictions for eighteen years, and I believe politicians go through deep withdrawal when they lose. They fear the loss of an election more than anything else.

Here is where we come in. We take control with the help of the Internet and tell them to stop listening to the lobbyists and start listening to us. If they don't, it won't matter how much the lobbyists give them because they will be out of office.

It's the sad truth that more people *don't* vote than do. The most powerful tool we have is our vote and right now the politicians are getting very nervous because the so-called minorities are becoming the majority, and they are organizing themselves and *voting*. This tells you something and proves just how powerful we all are.

Schools should be required to teach about positive and negative energy at all levels. Everyone should be taught, and shown, how to think positive—"how can I make things better?" Quantum physics would be understood by all, so religion would take a new form. Being spiritual would mean growing up on a planet being a positive person in everything you do. All of the great enlightened beings like Buddha and Jesus, were trying to tell us this, but others always found a way to turn that attitude into power and money and ultimately distorted the teachings of those great beings.

Ever wonder why the media doesn't follow through on certain stories? Most of the time it's because it doesn't fit their agenda, so we are fed 'fresh' news. It's ironic, because the fresh news is really more of the same with a different headline. Mass media is controlled by power brokers, all with an agenda, and they use the news as a way of controlling us and keeping us in fear. If we fear, we won't act, and if we don't act, they control us.

To become more aware and enlightened, read anything by Eckhart Tolle and Michael A. Singers book, The Untethered Soul. Become more informed about Quantum Physics. This is easy to do by reading The Secret. Thich Nhat Hanh's book Going Home is very informative. The point is question why, don't just accept what you are told. The answer is simple; just how did we get this way and now how do we fix it.

Is there a planet Plytar? Probably not.

Is there a magic transformation essence? Almost certainly not.

But the world still has a chance. It's up to us to change it. *Victor Rugg*

About the Author

Victor Rugg has a BA and MPA from Long Island University where he also was an adjunct Professor. He first worked for Johnson and Johnson and then spent 15 years working for Suffolk County Government in New York, where he also served as the Acting Commissioner of the Department of Drug and Alcohol Services. He started Spector Graphics, a photography, sign, and graphics company based in East Hampton with 45 outlets across the country. He has invented a number of tools. An avid sailor, he sailed for 13 months from Tortola to Venezuela and back to Palm Beach Gardens, Florida. Today, he is a professional photographer. His works can be seen in Galleries, Books, Magazines, the Internet and Newspapers. He has never stopped studying Mind, Body and Spirit and world economics. His poem, 'A Trace', received an Outstanding Achievement Award from the International Library of Poetry.

Photo by Edith Ingenhaag

Randy Cribbs is an award winning author of nine other books, including 'The Vessel: Tinaja, An Ancient City Mystery' and 'Ghosts, Another Summer in the Old Town. For more info, go to www.randycribbsauthor.com.

CPSIA information can be obtained at www.ICGtesting.com
Printed in the USA
LVOW12s0526070814

397887LV00002B/3/P